"Maybe we should put the word out that we're here. It could put off someone sending hired guns to the ranch."

He pulled back, met her gaze. "And make ourselves targets. Especially you." Owen cursed softly. "You're thinking of Addie. Thank you for that."

"You don't have to thank me. Of course I'm thinking about her, and I'd rather thugs come after me here than there. In fact, maybe it's time to use me as bait."

This time, his profanity wasn't so soft, and he jerked away. "No," he snapped. "No." When he repeated it, his voice was a little softer, but it was filled with just as much emotion. "And that doesn't have a damn thing to do with that kiss. Or this one."

Laney didn't even see it coming, but his mouth was suddenly on hers.

A THREAT TO HIS FAMILY

USA TODAY Bestselling Author

DELORES FOSSEN

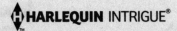
HARLEQUIN INTRIGUE®

Recycling programs
for this product may
not exist in your area.

ISBN-13: 978-1-335-13621-3

A Threat to His Family

Copyright © 2019 by Delores Fossen

Printed in U.S.A.

Delores Fossen, a *USA TODAY* bestselling author, has written over one hundred novels, with millions of copies of her books in print worldwide. She's received a Booksellers' Best Award and an RT Reviewers' Choice Best Book Award. She was also a finalist for a prestigious RITA® Award. You can contact the author through her website at www.deloresfossen.com.

Books by Delores Fossen

Visit the Author Profile page at Harlequin.com.

CAST OF CHARACTERS

Deputy Owen Slater—This Texas lawman has already lost his wife in childbirth, but a new threat puts him in the path of a vicious killer and forces him to confront feelings that he's not sure he's ready to face.

Laney Martin—She manages Owen's ranch, but she's also trying to track down the person who murdered her sister. Owen can help with that, but Laney hadn't counted on the intense attraction to the lawman who could unknowingly be sheltering a killer.

Addie Slater—Owen's daughter. She's only eighteen months old and too young to understand that she could be in danger.

Emerson Keaton—Longview Ridge's district attorney and Owen's former brother-in-law. He has secrets, and one of those secrets could put Owen's and Laney's lives on the line.

Nettie Keaton—Emerson's socialite wife, who might go to any lengths to protect her marriage and her husband's image.

Terrance McCoy—A wealthy businessman who's on probation for assaulting Laney. It's no secret that he hates her, but does he also want her dead?

about her mom a half hour ago." While her voice was level enough for him to understand her, each word had come through her panting breaths. "Francine asked me to watch Addie while she went over there to check on her."

Francine's mom had dementia so it wasn't unusual for the nanny to get calls about her. However, this was the first time she'd left Addie with Laney. Maybe, though, Francine had done that because she'd known Owen would soon be home.

An intruder who'd been watching the place would have known that, too.

"Who's in the house?" he asked.

Another head shake from Laney. "A man."

Not that he needed it, but Owen had more confirmation of the danger. He saw that Laney had a gun, a small snub-nosed .38. It didn't belong to him, nor was it one that he'd ever seen in the guesthouse where Laney was staying. Later, he'd ask her about it, about why she hadn't mentioned that she had a weapon, but for now they obviously had a much bigger problem.

Owen texted this brother again, to warn him about the intruder so that Kellan didn't walk into a situation that could turn deadly. He also asked Kellan to call in more backup. If the person upstairs started shooting, Owen wanted all the help he could get.

"What happened?" Owen whispered to Laney.

She opened her mouth, paused and then closed it as if she'd changed her mind about what to say.

"About ten minutes ago, I was in the kitchen with Addie when the power went off. A few seconds later, a man came in through the front door and I hid in the pantry with her until he went upstairs."

Smart thinking on Laney's part to hide instead of panicking or confronting the guy. But it gave Owen an uneasy feeling that Laney could think that fast under such pressure. And then there was the gun again. Where had she gotten it? The guesthouse was on the other side of the backyard, much farther away than the barn. If she'd gone to the guesthouse to get the gun, why hadn't she just stayed there with Addie? It would have been safer than running across the yard with the baby.

"Did you get a good look at the man?" Owen prompted.

Laney again shook her head. "But I heard him. When he stepped into the house, I knew it wasn't you, so I guessed it must be trouble."

Again, quick thinking on her part. He wasn't sure why, though, that gave him a very uneasy feeling.

"I didn't hear or see a vehicle," Laney added.

Owen hadn't seen one, either, which meant the guy must have come on foot. Not impossible, but Owen's ranch was a good half mile from the main road. If this was a thief, he wasn't going to get away with much. Plus, it would be damn brazen of some idiot to break into a cop's home just to commit a robbery.

So what was really going on?

The tight knot in Owen's gut told him it would be needed.

And Kellan was the best backup Owen could ask for. Not only was he the sheriff of their hometown of Longview Ridge, he lived just two miles away. Kellan could be there in no time.

Using his elbow, Owen nudged the door open all the way and glanced around. His house had an open floor plan, so with a single sweeping glance, he could take in the living room, kitchen and dining area. Or at least he could have done that had it not been so blasted dark. There were way too many shadows. Too many places for someone to hide.

Owen flipped the light switch. Nothing. That snowballed the wildfire concerns because it meant someone could have cut off the power to the house. He doubted this was some kind of electric malfunction because if it had been, Francine would have gotten out the candles and flashlights since she was well aware of Addie's fear of the dark.

Even though his brother would be here in minutes, Owen didn't want to wait for him. The thought of his baby hurt and scared got him moving. With a two-handed grip on his gun, he checked behind the sofa, making sure he continued to keep watch. No one was there, so he moved to the dining room. Still no one.

But he heard something.

There were footsteps upstairs. Not Addie's toddling feet, either. These were heavy and slow, probably the way his own steps would sound if he were up there looking around. Owen turned to head in that direction in case it was Francine, but that was when he noticed the back door was open, too. And there were sounds coming from the yard.

"Shh," someone whispered. "We need to play the quiet game."

Because the voice was so ragged, it took Owen a moment to realize it was Laney Martin, his ranch manager. That sent him hurrying straight to the door, and he saw Laney running toward the barn. She had Addie clutched to her chest, her hand cupping the back of the baby's head.

Owen didn't call out to them, but he did catch a glimpse of Laney's face as they ducked into the barn. She was terrified. He hadn't needed anything to up his own level of fear, but that did it. He ran across the yard and went straight into the barn. He heard another sound. Laney's sharp gasp.

"It's me," Owen whispered just in case she thought it was someone else who'd followed them in there.

Laney had already moved to the far corner of the barn next to a stack of hay bales. When she shifted her position, Owen could see his baby's face. Addie was smiling as if this were indeed a fun game. It was good that she was too young to realize the danger they were in.

"Where's Francine?" he asked. "Is she in the house?"

Laney shook her head. "The nursing home called

Owen glanced around the barn, also keeping watch on the yard in case the intruder followed them out here. Part of him wanted that to happen so he could make the piece of dirt pay for putting Addie and Laney through this.

There were no ranch hands around that he could see. Not a surprise. He ran a small operation and only had three full-time hands and Laney, who managed the place. Other than Laney, none of the others lived on the grounds. Not even Francine, since she had her own house only a couple of miles away.

He glanced at the light switch and considered turning it off, but that might only make things worse. If the intruder saw it, he would know they were in the barn, and he might come out there with guns blazing.

Owen's phone dinged with a text message from Kellan.

I'm here, parked just up the road from your truck. Where is he?

Owen texted back.

Still in the house, I think.

But the moment he fired off the message, Owen saw something in the back doorway of the house. The moonlight glinted off metal and he caught a glimpse of the gun. That confirmed his worst fears, though he couldn't actually see the person holding the weapon. That was because he was likely dressed in all black and staying in the shadows.

Owen ducked back to avoid the barn light. That light probably helped Addie since she wasn't fretting as she usually did in the dark, but it might seem like a beacon to some thug looking to start trouble.

"Stay down," Owen instructed Laney. "I'll see if I can draw this guy out into the open—"

"You could be shot," she said before he even finished, her voice shaking.

Yeah, he could be, but if anyone was going to become a target, Owen wanted it to be him. He didn't want any shots fired into the barn or anywhere near Addie.

He texted Kellan to let him know that he was about to head out the back of the barn. He could then use the corral fence and nearby shrubs for cover to circle around the house.

Keep watch of the front, Owen added to the text.

He didn't intend to let this joker get away. He wanted to know who he was and why he'd broken in.

Owen eased the barn door shut and moved a saddle in front of it to block it. It wouldn't stop anyone for long, which was why he had to hurry. He ran to the back of the barn and climbed out through the opening sometimes used to push hay into the corral. When his feet hit the ground, he took a quick look around him.

No one.

No sounds, either. If the intruder was coming their way, he was being quiet about it. Owen tried to do the same as he made his way to the front side of the barn to take a look at the back porch.

Owen cursed.

The guy with the gun was no longer in sight, but the door was still open. Maybe he'd stepped back into the shadows to look for them. But that didn't make sense, either. By now, the intruder must have spotted Owen's truck, which was rigged with a police siren, and would have known that he had called for backup. That meant he possibly could have already fled the scene.

His phone dinged again with a text message. Owen was about to look down at the screen when he heard a sound he didn't want to hear.

A gunshot cracked through the air.

It didn't go into the part of the barn where Laney and Addie were, thank God, but it did slam into the wood right next to where Owen was standing. That forced him to move back. And to wait. He didn't have to wait long. However, this time it wasn't another shot. It was a man's voice.

"Elaine?" a man yelled. "I know you're out there."

Owen had no idea who this Elaine was, so maybe this was a case of the thug showing up at the wrong place.

Except, wasn't Laney a nickname for Elaine?

Was this man someone from Laney's past? Maybe an old boyfriend who'd come to settle a score?

If so, she'd never mentioned it and nothing had shown up about relationship issues in the background check he'd run on her, and he'd been pretty darn thorough since Laney would be living so close to Addie and him. While he continued to volley glances all around him, Owen checked his phone screen and saw the text from Kellan.

I'm moving to the right side of your house.

Good. There was a door there, just off the playroom. Maybe Kellan would be able to slip into the house and get a look at this guy. Or, better yet, arrest him.

"I'm Deputy Owen Slater," Owen called out. "Put down your weapon and come out with your hands up."

It was something that, as a cop, Owen needed to say. He had to identify himself in the hope it would cause the idiot to surrender. Of course, it was just as likely to cause him to fire more shots. If he did, Owen would be justified in using deadly force.

But no other shots. Just another shout.

"Elaine?" the man yelled again.

Owen used the sound of the man's voice to try to pinpoint his location. He was definitely no longer by the back door. Nowhere near it. This guy was in

Chapter One

Deputy Owen Slater knew something was wrong the moment he stopped his truck in front of his house.

There were no lights on, not even the ones on the porch or in the upstairs window of the nursery. It was just a little past eight and that meant it was his daughter Addie's bedtime, but she always slept with the lamp on.

If the electricity had gone off, the nanny, Francine Landry, would have almost certainly texted Owen to let him know. Besides, Owen had already spotted a light in the barn. That wasn't unusual since the light was often left on there, but it meant the power definitely wasn't out.

Because he was both a father and a cop, the bad thoughts came and his pulse kicked up hard and fast. Something had maybe gone wrong. Over the years, he'd made plenty of arrests, and it could be that someone wanted to get back at him. A surefire way to do that was to come here to his home, to a place where he thought he and his child were safe.

The panic came, shooting through him when he thought of his daughter being in danger. Addie was only eighteen months old, just a baby. He'd already lost her mother in childbirth and he couldn't lose Addie, too.

That got Owen drawing his gun as he started running. He fired glances all around him in case this was an ambush, but no one came at him as he barreled up the porch steps.

Hell.

The front door was slightly ajar. That was another indication that something wasn't right. Francine always kept things locked up tight now that Addie was walking and had developed some escape skills.

Owen didn't call out to Francine, something he desperately wanted to do with the hope he'd hear her say that everything was okay. But if he called out, it could alert someone other than the nanny. Still, he prayed that she would come rushing in to give him some account for what was happening. But no good explanation came to mind.

Owen tried to rein in his heartbeat and breathing. Hard to do, though, when the stakes were this high, but he forced himself to remember his training and experience. That meant requesting backup before he started a search of the area. He quickly texted his brother Kellan to get there ASAP so he'd have some help if needed.

the guesthouse, where Laney lived. How he'd gotten there, Owen didn't know, but it was possible that he'd climbed through a window.

Since the intruder was now on the same side of the yard as Owen, it made him an easy target, and that was why he hurried back into the barn. He glanced at Laney. Or rather, where he'd last seen Addie and her, but Laney had moved a few feet. She had positioned herself behind the hay bales and was using one as support for her shooting hand.

"Where's the baby?" Owen immediately asked.

"On the floor behind me. She's playing with my necklace. I wanted to be between the door and her in case… Well, just in case," Laney added.

Just in case wasn't looking very good right now. But at least they were all still safe. He heard Addie then, and she wasn't fussing. It was more of a cooing babble, so the necklace must have been holding her attention.

"Elaine?" the man called out. He had moved since his last shout, but Owen wasn't sure to where. He also wasn't sure of Laney's reaction.

The color had blanched from her face and he didn't think it was because of the danger. Owen didn't have to be a cop to figure out what that meant.

"You know this guy," he said.

She didn't deny it, causing Owen to curse under his breath.

"What does he want with you?" Owen demanded.

She didn't get a chance to answer him because the man shouted again. "Elaine, let's do this the easy way. Come out now and leave with me, and no one will get hurt."

Hell. There was a good bit of anger now mixed with fear for his daughter. Anger that this thug would try to bargain like this. No way was Owen going to let Laney leave with a man who'd just fired a shot at him.

"Watch out!" someone yelled. Not the thug this time. It was Kellan. "He's coming right at you."

That wasn't the only thing that came, either. There was a gunshot, quickly followed by another one. From the sound of it, the second shot had come from a different weapon.

Maybe Kellan's.

Owen hoped it had anyway. Because he didn't like the odds if this intruder had brought his own version of backup with him.

He debated opening the barn door so he could help his brother, but since this guy was likely coming for them, Owen's top priority was to make sure that Addie was protected. He hurried to Laney and Addie, standing guard in front of them and waiting for whatever was about to happen.

Owen didn't have to wait long. Someone kicked the barn door hard, and bits of wood went flying. The saddle shifted, too, and Owen steeled himself to fire. He was about to do that when he got a glimpse of the person who'd just broken down the door. The man, dressed in black, took aim at them. However, before Owen could pull the trigger, shots blasted through the barn.

Laney had fired.

And she hadn't missed.

The bullets, first one and then the other, slammed into the man's chest and he dropped to the ground like a stone. If he wasn't dead, he soon would be, because he was already bleeding out.

Addie started to cry so Owen hurried to her. The relief came flooding through him because his baby was okay. She hadn't been hurt.

He didn't scoop her up into his arms, something he desperately wanted to do. First, he had to wait for the all clear from Kellan, and that might take a couple of minutes. In the meantime, Owen would need to hold his position. However, that didn't stop him from asking one critical question.

Owen's eyes narrowed when he looked at Laney. "Start talking. Who the heck are you?"

Chapter Two

From the moment this nightmare had started, Laney had known that question—and many more—would come from Owen.

Who the heck are you?

No way would Owen Slater just let something like this go. Of course, he probably thought her answer would help him understand this mess. It wouldn't. In fact, it was going to make things even worse.

At least he and Addie hadn't been hurt. And the toddler was so young that she hopefully wouldn't remember anything about this attack. However, the assault would stay with Owen for the rest of his life, and Laney was never going to be able to forgive herself for allowing things to come to this.

Sweet heaven. She could have gotten them killed.

With his scalpel-sharp glare, Owen reminded her that he was well aware of that, too. In fact, the only reason he likely didn't take Addie from Laney when she picked up the baby was that he needed to keep his shooting hand free in case someone else fired at them.

She glanced at the man she'd just shot. Who the heck was he? How had he known who she was? And why had he done this? He hadn't given her any choice, but it still twisted away at her. A man was dying or already dead because of her. And worse, this wasn't over. If she'd managed to somehow keep him alive, he might have been coerced into telling her who'd put him up to this, but she'd had no choice but to take that shot.

"Who are you?" Owen repeated.

Judging from the tone and his intense glare, he no longer trusted her. Good. Because Laney didn't trust herself.

It crushed her to have it all come to this. She'd thought she was safe, that Addie and Owen would be safe, too. Obviously she'd brought her fight right to their doorstep.

"I was Elaine Pearce," she said, speaking around the lump in her throat, "but I changed my name to Laney Martin."

Of course, that explanation was just the tip of the iceberg. Owen would demand to know about not only the name change, but also how it connected to the dead man. And how it connected to this attack.

Owen sent a text to someone. Probably to one of his fellow deputies to do a quick background check on Elaine Pearce. It was what Laney would have done had their positions been reversed.

"I want you to put your gun on the hay bale," he instructed. He sounded like a cop now, and he looked at her as if she were a criminal.

Laney did exactly as he said, knowing the gun would be taken as part as of the evidence in what was now a crime scene. An investigation would quickly follow, which meant she'd be questioned and re-questioned. Soon, everyone in town would know who she was, and she'd be in more danger than she already was. That was why she had to figure a way out of here—fast.

"Elaine Pearce," he repeated. "And you didn't think that was something I should know?" Owen grumbled. "You didn't bother to mention that you weren't who you were claiming to be?"

"No." Laney took another deep breath. "I thought I'd find the info that I needed and be out of here before anything could happen."

"You were obviously wrong about that." He gave a disapproving grunt and went to the man, kicking his gun farther away from where it had fallen from the shooter's hand. Owen then touched his fingers to the guy's neck.

"Dead," Owen relayed as he did a quick search of the guy's pockets. Nothing. Of course, he hadn't expected a hired gun to bring an actual ID with him.

"You recognize him?" Owen asked.

Laney somehow managed to stand upright, though every part of her was trembling. She also moved closer to Owen and then made another quick check on Addie. The little girl's cries were already starting to taper off, but she'd obviously been frightened by the noise of the gunshots.

A muscle tightened in Owen's jaw and, though Laney hadn't thought it possible, his steel-gray eyes narrowed even more when he glared at her. He made a circling motion with his index finger for her to continue, but before Laney even had the chance to do that, his phone rang. She saw his brother's name on the screen. In the months that she'd been working for Owen, she'd met Kellan several times and knew he lived close by. She had figured Owen had called him or their other brothers for backup.

"This conversation isn't over," Owen assured her as he hit the answer button on his phone. He didn't put the call on speaker, but Laney was close enough to hear Kellan's voice.

"There's a second intruder," Kellan blurted out, causing a chill to ripple through her.

Laney hurried back to Addie and pulled the little girl into her arms. Because of her position, she could no longer hear what Kellan was saying. But judging from the way Owen's gaze fired around, he, too, was bracing himself for another attack. He didn't stay on the phone long and, once he was finished with his conversation, maneuvered himself in front of them.

"The second guy was in the guesthouse," Owen told her. "He ran into the woods across the road. Kellan and Gunnar are searching for him now and they've called Dispatch for more backup."

Gunnar was Deputy Gunnar Pullam, someone else that Laney had seen around town. Like Owen, he was an experienced lawman. Something they needed right now. Maybe they'd find the second man and stop him from circling back to try to kill them again. The thought didn't help with her heartbeat, which was already thudding out of control. Addie must have picked up on that, too, because she started to whimper again. Laney began to rock her.

"Kellan said the second man had something with him when he ran out of the guesthouse," Owen went on. "A bag, maybe." His back was to her now, but she didn't need to see his face to know he was still glaring. "Any idea what he took?"

Laney's thoughts were all over the place as she tried to fight off the panic, but it didn't take her long to come up with an answer. "Maybe my toothbrush or something else with my DNA on it. Something to prove who I am."

Other than changing her hair and wearing colored contacts, she hadn't altered her appearance that much. If they'd looked closely enough, whoever was after her could have recognized her from old photos she was certain were still out there on the web. But a hired gun would have wanted some kind of proof to give to his boss and DNA would have done it.

That didn't feel right, though.

She fought through the whirlwind of thoughts and spiked adrenaline, and remembered that one of the intruders had called her by her real name. Elaine. And the one she'd killed had come into the barn to either take her with him or gun her down. So maybe they hadn't been looking for someone to prove who she was. Maybe they'd been after something else in the guesthouse and the man she'd shot had been just a distraction for his partner.

"My laptop," she added on a rise of breath. Though everything on it was password protected or stored on a cloud with several layers of security, a good hacker would be able to find what she had there.

"Keep talking," Owen ordered her while he continued volleying glances between the front door and the window at the back. "Why'd you lie to me about who you were?"

Again, this would only lead to more questions, but she doubted that she could stall Owen, especially since the sense of danger was still so thick around them.

"I lied because I didn't want anyone, including you, to know my real identity." Laney paused when her breath suddenly became very thin. "I'm working on an investigation, and the clues led me here to Longview Ridge."

Owen pulled back his shoulders. "Are you a cop?"

"A private investigator."

Owen growled out some profanity under his breath and looked as if he wanted to do more than growl it. He'd kept it quiet, no doubt because his daughter was right there, but thankfully Addie was falling asleep, her head now resting on Laney's shoulder.

"So, you're a PI and a liar," Owen rumbled. Obviously he didn't think much of either. "I obviously missed way too much about you when I did your background check. And now you've put my little girl, me and now Gunner and my brother in danger."

Yes. She'd done all of those things and more. "I'm investigating Emerson Keaton."

She saw the brief moment of surprise, followed by a new round of silent profanity that went through his eyes. "My brother-in-law. Addie's uncle."

Laney could add another mental *yes* to that. Emerson was indeed both of those things, along with being the town's district attorney. She was also convinced that he had a fourth label.

Killer.

Of course, there was no way Owen would believe that, and she wasn't going to be able to convince him of it now. Laney couldn't blame him for his doubts. Nearly everything she'd told him had been a lie, including the résumé and references she'd manufactured to get this job.

Owen's intense stare demanded that she continue even though they obviously still had to keep watch.

"Seven months ago, my half sister was murdered. Hadley Odom." Laney had said Hadley's name around the thick lump in her throat. "We were close."

Not a lie. They had been, despite the different ways they'd chosen to live their lives.

"What the heck does your half sister's murder have to do with Emerson?" Owen snapped.

"Everything," Laney managed to say, and she repeated it to give herself some extra time to gather her words and her breath. "Hadley and Emerson had an affair."

"Emerson?" Owen challenged when she paused. There was a bucket of skepticism in his tone. With good reason. Emerson was the golden boy of Longview Ridge. He had a beautiful wife, two young kids and a spotless reputation. "I've known Emerson my whole life, and there's never been a hint of him having an affair."

"He and Hadley kept it secret. Not just for Emerson's sake but for Hadley's. Hadley and I had the same mother, but her father, my stepfather, wouldn't have approved." Actually, Laney hadn't approved, either, but it was impossible to sway Hadley once she'd had her mind set on something.

Owen stayed quiet for a moment, his expression hard, ice-cold. "You have proof of this?"

"I heard Hadley talking to him on the phone, and I saw them together once when they were at a restaurant."

Of course, that wasn't proof she thought Owen was just going to accept. And she was right. Owen's scowl only worsened.

"Hadley told me they were having an affair." She spelled it out for him. "She also told me that she got very upset when he broke things off with her. In anger, Hadley threatened to tell his wife and, less than twelve hours later, she was dead."

"And you think Emerson killed her." It wasn't a question.

Owen wasn't believing any of this. Neither had anyone else she'd told, but Laney had plenty of proof that she was pushing the wrong buttons with her investigation.

She tipped her head to the dead man. "He came here after me. Why else would he do that if I weren't getting close to proving what Emerson did?"

Owen didn't roll his eyes, but it was close. Then he huffed, "If you're really a PI as you say you are, then I suspect you've riled some people. You've certainly done that to me."

"Yes, but you don't want me dead. Emerson does."

However, she had to mentally shake her head. Someone wanted to kill her and the most obvious suspect was the one she was investigating. But there was someone else and her expression must have let Owen know that.

"Remembering something else?" Owen snapped.

No way did she want to lie to him again, but before Laney could even begin to answer him, she heard footsteps outside the barn. That gave her another shot of adrenaline and she crouched again with Addie.

"It's me," someone said.

Kellan.

Not the threat her body had been geared up to face. However, like Owen, Kellan was scowling when he came into the barn. He glanced at his brother and niece. Then at the dead man. Then at Laney. She didn't think it was her imagination that she got the brunt of the scowl he was doling out.

"We got the second intruder," Kellan explained. "He's alive."

Laney released the breath she hadn't even known she'd been holding. "Who is he?" she blurted. "Has he said anything?"

"Oh, he's talking a lot," Kellan grumbled. "He's demanding to see you. He says he's a friend of yours, that you're the one who hired him."

"No." Laney couldn't deny that fast enough. "He's lying."

Judging from the flat look Kellan gave her, he wasn't buying it. Apparently, neither was Owen because he walked closer and took Addie from her. He immediately moved next to his brother.

"There's more," Kellan added a moment later. "The intruder says that you hired him to kill Owen."

Chapter Three

Owen hadn't wanted to spend half the night in the sheriff's office, where he spent most of his days, but he hadn't had a choice. This was not just a simple B and E, and with the shooting death of one of the intruders, it was a tangled mess.

One not likely to be resolved before morning.

That was because Laney had denied hiring the intruder, and the intruder was insisting he was telling the truth. That put them at a temporary stalemate. Or at least it would have if Owen had any faith in the intruder. Hard to trust someone who'd come to his home and broken in while his baby daughter had been there. Of course, the reason the intruder had come was Laney.

That meant this was another stalemate.

One that he hoped to break soon.

There was an entire CSI team going through his place, which meant he wouldn't be going home tonight. The only silver lining was that Francine had

taken Addie to her place. Not alone, either. Owen
had sent Gunnar with them just case this "mess" got
another layer to it with a second attack.

In the meantime, Owen had been in the mind-
set of collecting as much information as he could
through phone conversations and emails. He hadn't
done all of that under Laney's watchful eyes and
alert ears, either. He'd left her in his office for some
of those calls and was now trying to process everything he'd learned.

Laney hadn't been idle, either. She'd made a call,
too. With a cheap, disposable cell phone, he'd noticed. And Owen had made sure he kept his ears alert
during her conversation. She'd spoken to someone
she called Joe and told him to be careful.

That was it.

The chat had lasted less than five seconds and
then Laney had immediately surrendered the phone
to Owen. Not that it had been of any use to him since
Joe hadn't answered when Owen had tried to call
him. Laney had briefly—*very briefly*—explained
that Joe Henshaw was her assistant, and that she
didn't know where he was. Neither did Owen or the
San Antonio cops helping him look for the guy.

"I didn't hire that man to kill you," Laney repeated when Owen finished his latest call, this one
to the medical examiner.

Declaring and redeclaring her innocence was
something Laney had been going on about during

the entire five hours they'd been there. He suspected she would continue to go on about it until the intruder either recanted or Kellan and he were indeed able to prove that he was lying.

Owen figured proving it wouldn't be that hard.

However, they couldn't even start doing that because the guy had lawyered up and they now had to wait for the attorney to arrive from San Antonio. Until then, they were holding not only the intruder but also Laney. Owen had not yet decided if she was a suspect, but he was pretty sure Laney—or rather Elaine—was going to be the key to them figuring out what the hell was going on.

"The guy you shot and killed was Harvey Dayton," Owen told her. He'd just gotten the ID during his call with the ME. "Ring any bells?"

"No," she answered without hesitation. "And I'm sure I've never seen him before, either. His prints were in the system," Laney added in a mutter. "That's how you got the ID this fast?"

He nodded. "Dayton had a record," Owen settled for saying.

What he didn't spell out for her was that the rap sheet was a mile long, and yeah, it included a couple of assault charges with a pattern of escalating violence. Along with a history of drug use, which made him a prime candidate for becoming a hired gun for people who wanted cheap help.

"Did Dayton say what he took from the guest-house?" Laney asked.

Good question because, other than a gun, Dayton hadn't had anything on him when Kellan and Gunnar had found him. The CSIs would search the area, but Dayton had been captured by the road, a good quarter mile from Owen's ranch. There was no telling where he'd put whatever it was he'd taken.

"Your laptop is missing," Owen added, and he instantly saw the frustration and anger in her eyes.

"I keep copies of my files in online storage," she said with a heavy sigh. "But everything was also on my hard drive. It means whoever took it won't have trouble accessing everything."

Later, he'd want to know more about exactly what was on it. For now, Owen went with giving her more info that would then lead to more questions. Hopefully, more answers, too. "Your toothbrush was there, so that axes your DNA theory. Your purse was open, and your wallet and cell phone were gone. No jewelry around, either, so if you had any—"

"The only jewelry I have is this." Laney touched her fingers to the gold dragonfly necklace that she'd gotten back from Addie. There was also a small key on the chain. "It was a gift from my sister." She paused. "You really think the motive for this was robbery?"

"No." Owen didn't have to think about that.

The gunman had called her by name and come to

the barn. Plus, nothing was missing from his house. If this had been a robbery, they would have taken his wallet and anything else of value. They also would have had a vehicle stashed nearby, and so far, one hadn't turned up.

"And the second man, the one who's lying about me, any ID on him yet?" she queried.

"Rohan Gilley." Owen watched for any signs of recognition.

She repeated the name several times, the way a person would when they were trying to jog their memory. But then Laney shook her head. "He had a record, too?"

Owen settled for a nod. Gilley's rap sheet was almost identical to Dayton's, just slightly shorter. They'd even served time together.

"Gilley's lying to save his hide," Laney grumbled. "Or because someone put him up to it." She added some muttered profanity to go along with that.

The last five hours hadn't improved her mood much. She was just as wired as she had been during the attack. At least, though, she wasn't trembling now. For reasons he didn't want to explore, the trembling got to Owen, and right now the only thing he wanted to feel for this woman was the cool indifference he felt toward anyone who'd been involved in any way with a crime.

But indifference was impossible.

If she was telling the truth about not hiring

Gilley—and he believed that she was—then that meant she was a victim, one who'd saved his daughter by getting her out of harm's way. Hard for something that big not to be on the proverbial table.

Laney's tough exterior, or rather the front she'd tried to put on for him, cracked a little. She didn't go back to trembling, but it was close, and before she could gather her composure, he caught another glimpse of nerves.

Big ones.

She was a PI—he'd confirmed that—but this could have been the first time she'd actually been in the middle of an attack. Maybe the first time she had been a target, too.

Along with having a good aim, she had an athletic build and was on the petite side, only about five-three.

And attractive.

Something he hated that he noticed, but it was impossible to miss. Being a widower hadn't made him blind. However, he still had plenty of common sense that reminded him that Laney had way too many secrets behind those cool blue eyes.

"The CSIs found a jammer," Owen went on a moment later. "That's how Dayton and or Gilley cut off the electricity."

She stayed quiet for a moment. "That proves I'm innocent. I wouldn't have needed to jam the power since I was already in the house." Her eyes widened. "Did you check to make sure Francine really had an emergency? Those men wanted me there, and they could have tricked Francine into leaving."

At least Laney wasn't accusing the nanny of any wrongdoing, but it was a clever observation. An accurate one, too. "The call from the nursing home was bogus." Of course, Francine hadn't learned that until she'd gotten there to check on her mom. By then, the attack at the ranch had already been in progress.

"More proof," Laney said under her breath. She looked up, her eyes meeting his. "If I wanted you dead, I wouldn't have kept Addie there. I would have told Francine I couldn't watch the girl so that Francine would have had to take Addie with her."

That was the way Owen had it figured, too, which was why he was leaning toward the conclusion that Laney was innocent. Of the attack anyway. But there was a boatload of other troubling concerns here. Not just the lies that she'd told him about her identity and work résumé, but there was also the problem with the accusation about Emerson.

"Go back over what you told me in the barn," Owen insisted. "Tell me about your half sister's murder."

This would be a third round of Laney doing that, but thanks to an emailed report he'd gotten from the San Antonio PD in the past hour, Owen knew that Hadley's death had indeed been ruled a murder.

She'd died from blunt-force trauma to the head. No eyewitnesses, no suspects. Well, no official suspects for SAPD. Laney clearly felt differently about that.

"Hadley and Emerson had an affair." Laney stared at him. "I'm not going to change my story, no matter how many times you have me repeat it."

That was what he figured, but this was another square filler, like calling out his identity to the intruder. It was especially necessary because she'd lied to him about who she was.

Something that still riled him to the core.

Hell, here he was a cop, and he hadn't known one of his employees was living under an alias. Of course, there was no way he would have hired her had he known who she was and what she was after. That got Owen thinking—exactly what was she after anyway?

"Did you think I was covering up about my brother-in-law?" he asked.

"Yes." Her answer came quickly, causing him to huff. If she truly believed Emerson had murdered her sister, then she'd just accused Owen of assorted felonies by not reporting the crime and obstructing justice. An accusation she must have realized because her gaze darted away. "I know you're close to him."

Yeah, he was. Emerson had helped him get through Naomi's death. Those days had been so dark, Owen would have slid right down into the deepest, darkest hole if it hadn't been for Addie and Emerson.

Of course, Emerson had been grieving, too, since he'd lost his only sister that day. Naomi and Emerson had been close, and while Owen didn't have the deep connection with Emerson that Naomi had, Owen respected the man, especially after Naomi's death when Emerson and he had been drawn together in grief. Maybe "misery loves company" had worked for both of them. Though there were times when Owen wondered if anything had actually worked. The grief could still slice through him.

"Tell me why you think Emerson killed Hadley," Owen demanded. "And stick to only what you can prove. Gut feelings don't count here."

Her mouth tightened a little. "Hadley told me it got ugly when her relationship with Emerson was over. Like I said, she threatened to tell his wife, and then Emerson threatened her. He said he'd hurt her if she didn't keep her mouth shut."

Emerson could have a hot head. Owen had even been on the receiving end of one of his punches in high school when they'd disagreed over the score in a pick-up basketball game. But it was a big stretch to go from a punch to hurting a woman, much less killing her.

"That isn't proof," Owen quickly pointed out. "It's hearsay."

Laney didn't dodge his gaze this time. "I have pictures."

That got his attention. There'd been nothing about that in the police report. "Pictures?" he challenged.

She nodded. "Of Emerson and Hadley together." Another pause, then she mumbled something he didn't catch. "Hadley told me about them and said she kept them in a safe-deposit box."

Owen wasn't sure what to react to first. That there could be pictures or that this was the first he was hearing about it. "And you didn't bother to tell the cops that?" he snarled.

"I did tell them, but I didn't know where they were. Hadley hadn't given me the name of the bank where she had the box." Her forehead bunched up. "I didn't ask, either, because I didn't know how important those pictures were going to become."

"They still might not be important. If the photos exist, they could possibly be proof of an affair and nothing more." Though it twisted at his insides to think Emerson could have cheated on his wife.

Laney made a sound of disagreement. "They're important. Because they're the first step in proving that Emerson carried through on his threat to hurt her."

Owen glanced at the key on the chain around her neck and groaned. "That's for the safe-deposit box?"

Her response wasn't so quick this time. "Yes, I believe it is. And I'll give it to the cops when I find out which bank has the photos. By cops, I mean the

San Antonio Police, not anyone who has a personal connection to Emerson."

Of course. Laney wouldn't trust him with the key because she believed he would tip off Emerson. Or destroy the pictures.

He wouldn't.

If Owen did find something like that, he would do his job. But he doubted he could convince Laney of that. Doubted, too, that he could convince her of anything else right now.

"If there are photos and a safe-deposit box, they could be anywhere," he pointed out. "You need help finding them… Joe Henshaw's helping you with that."

She nodded. "He's a PI, too, and we became friends in a grief support group. He lost both his parents when they were murdered. Sorry," Laney added.

The apology was no doubt because his father had been murdered, too, about a year ago, not long after Owen had lost his wife. His father had been gunned down by an unknown perp who was still out there. Owen had hope, though, that the case would be solved since they had an eyewitness. Too bad the witness had received a head injury and couldn't remember squat about what had happened. But maybe one day she would remember.

One day.

Even though it had nearly killed Owen to lose Naomi, it was a deeper cut to lose his father. Naomi's death had been a medical problem. A blood clot that had formed during delivery. But his dad's life had been purposely taken. Murdered. And all of Owen's skills learned in training as a cop hadn't been able to stop it. Or bring the killer to justice.

Owen pushed that all aside, as he usually did when it came to his father, and went to the next item he needed to discuss with Laney.

"Tell me about Terrance McCoy."

She raked her finger over her eyebrow and shifted her posture a little. "SAPD told you about the restraining order." That was all she said for several moments. But yes, they had. "Then you also know that Terrance was a former client who wasn't happy with the outcome of an investigation I did for him."

That was a lukewarm explanation of a situation that had gotten pretty intense. Apparently, Terrance had hired Laney to do a thorough background check on a woman he'd met on an online dating site. When Laney hadn't turned up any red flags, Terrance had continued to see the woman, who ultimately swindled him out of a sizable chunk of his trust fund. He blamed Laney for that and had even accused her of being in cahoots with the swindler. No proof of that, though.

"Terrance assaulted you," Owen reminded her, letting her know what info he'd been given about the restraining order. "And he's been out of jail for weeks now. He could have hired those men who came after you tonight."

She looked him in the eyes again when she agreed with him. "Yes, and Joe is looking for Terrance now."

Apparently that had come up in the short conversation she'd had with Joe. Or maybe Joe agreed that Terrance was definitely a person of interest here.

"The San Antonio cops are looking for Terrance, too," Owen added.

After what had just happened, Terrance was at the top of their list of suspects. Ditto for anyone else Laney might have rubbed the wrong way. There were maybe other former clients out there. Dangerous ones. And because of the danger to Laney, Owen wasn't going to forget that Addie had been put in danger, too.

"I hate to ask, because I know it's just going to rile you even more than you already are," Laney said, "but could this be about your father?"

Yes, he'd considered it. Briefly. And then he'd dismissed it, and Owen was pretty sure the dismissal had been objective. Hard to be completely objective when it came to that kind of raw grief, but he thought he'd managed it.

"I'll be investigating all angles," Owen assured her. But he'd be looking especially hard at any of those directly connected to Laney.

Laney and Owen both glanced up when there was

movement in the doorway of his office. She practically jumped to her feet when she saw their visitor.

Emerson.

The man was wearing a rumpled suit, sporting some dark stubble and equally dark circles beneath his eyes. Emerson looked about as happy to be there as Owen was.

It probably wasn't a surprise to Laney that Owen had called his brother-in-law. Nor was it a surprise that Emerson had come. It'd taken him a couple of hours to get there because he'd had to drive in from Austin where he'd been away on a business trip.

Emerson frowned at Laney after sparing her only a glance, and then he looked at Owen. "Please tell me you have her accusations cleared up by now so I can go home and get some sleep."

"He hasn't cleared it up." Laney jumped in to answer before Owen could respond.

Emerson gave a weary sigh and rubbed his hand over his face. "Has she given you any proof whatsoever?" he asked.

Owen went still. It was a simple enough question, but it didn't feel like the right thing to say. He would have preferred to hear Emerson belt out a denial, tacking on some outrage that anyone was accusing him of cheating on his wife. There was something else that bothered him, too.

"You know Laney?" Owen asked him. "Elaine,"

he corrected. He waited because he had already seen the recognition in Emerson's eyes.

"I know her," Emerson stormed. "She's the PI who pestered me with calls about her sister. I told her to back off or I'd get a restraining order."

Arching his eyebrow, Owen shifted his attention to Laney and she acknowledged that with a nod. So, before tonight, Emerson had known about Laney's accusations, but he hadn't said a word about it to Owen. Something he should have done. Then again, maybe Emerson hadn't considered Laney enough of a credible threat.

"Emerson?" a woman called out, causing the man to groan.

Owen wasn't pleased, either, or especially surprised when Emerson's wife, Nettie, came hurrying through the front door, heading straight for them. "When you didn't answer your cell, I called the house, looking for you," Owen explained to Emerson. "Nettie answered, but I didn't tell her about Laney or the attack."

Emerson nodded and gave a resigned sigh. "Something like this won't stay quiet for long."

No. It wouldn't. And Nettie's expression was sporting a lot of concern. Ditto for the rest of her. Nettie was usually dressed to the nines, but tonight she was in yoga pants and a T-shirt. Her blond hair hadn't been combed and her eyes were red, as if she'd been crying.

"God, you're all right." Nettie threw herself into Emerson's arms. "I was so worried."

Owen glanced at Laney, and as expected, she was studying the couple. There was a different kind of worry and concern on her face. She was looking at them the way a cop would. No doubt to see if there were any signs that this was a marriage on the rocks because of a cheating husband. No signs, though. Emerson brushed a loving kiss on Nettie's forehead before he eased her away from him.

"Could you give Owen and me a minute alone?" Emerson asked his wife. "I won't be long. It's business."

Nettie studied him a moment and nodded before her attention went to Owen. Then Laney. There was no recognition in Nettie's icy gray eyes.

"I'll wait by the reception desk," Nettie said. She whispered something to Emerson, kissed him and then walked out of the office.

Emerson didn't do or say anything until his wife was out of earshot and then he tipped his head to Laney. "Anything she tells you about me is a lie, and I've wasted enough of my time dealing with her. Are you okay?" Emerson added to Owen. "Is Addie okay?"

Again, that bothered Owen. As Addie's uncle, it should have been the first thing for Emerson to ask. Of course, Owen had verified the okay status when he'd had a quick chat with Emerson earlier, so maybe Emerson thought that was enough.

But it wasn't. At least it didn't feel like it was.

Owen silently cursed. He hated that Laney had given him any doubts about Emerson. Especially since there was no proof.

"Addie's fine," Owen answered. "Francine said she would text me if Addie has any nightmares or such." Owen cursed that, too, but this time it wasn't silent. Because there could indeed be nightmares.

"I'll check on her first thing in the morning," Emerson volunteered. "Anything else you need or want me to do?"

Owen muttered his thanks and then nodded. "You'll have to make a statement about Laney's accusations."

Emerson gave another of those weary sighs. "I'll come by in the morning to do that, too."

Owen was about to ask him to go ahead and do it now. That way, Laney couldn't say that he'd given Emerson preferential treatment. Of course, she'd likely say that anyway. However, he didn't even get a chance to bring it up because Kellan appeared in the doorway. One look at his brother's face and Owen knew that something else was wrong.

"I just got off the phone with San Antonio PD," Kellan said, looking not at Emerson or Owen but at Laney. "They found your assistant, Joe Henshaw." Kellan paused. "He's dead."

Chapter Four

The shock felt to Laney like arctic ice covering her body. She blinked repeatedly—hoping she had misunderstood Kellan, that this was some kind of cop trick to unnerve her. But she knew from the look in his eyes that it was the truth.

"Oh, God." That was all she managed to say. There wasn't enough breath for her to add more, but the questions came immediately and started fighting their way through the veil of grief.

"How?" she mouthed.

Kellan's forehead bunched up, but he spoke the words fast. "He was murdered. Two gunshot wounds to the chest. That's all we know at this point because the ME has just started his examination."

Murdered. Joe had been murdered. The grief came, washing over her and going bone-deep.

"Joe's apartment had been ransacked," Kellan added a moment later. "Someone was obviously looking for something."

"Terrance," Laney rasped, though first, she had to swallow hard. "Joe was looking for him, and Terrance could have done this."

Since neither Owen or Kellan seemed surprised by that, she guessed they'd already come to the same conclusion. Good. If that snake was responsible, she wanted him to pay. But then if Terrance had killed Joe, he'd done it to get back at her.

She was responsible.

This time she wasn't able to choke back the sob and Laney clamped onto her bottom lip to make sure there wasn't another one. Sobs and tears wouldn't help now. Not when she needed answers. Later, when Owen and Kellan weren't around, she could fall apart.

"The San Antonio cops found him in his apartment," Kellan went on. "It appears someone broke in and killed him when he stepped from the shower. No defensive wounds, so it happened fast."

That last part was probably meant to comfort her. To let her know that Joe hadn't suffered. But in that instant, he would have seen his attacker and known he was about to die.

And all because of her.

Joe had not only been looking for Terrance, he'd also been looking for the safe-deposit box with those pictures. Someone had killed him because he'd been following her orders.

Laney groped around behind her to locate the

chair because she was afraid her legs were about to give way. Owen helped with that by taking hold of her arm to help her sit. He was studying her, maybe to gauge her reaction. That was when she glanced at Emerson, who was doing the same thing.

"I suppose you'll say I had something to do with this, too?" Emerson snapped, his words ripe with anger.

Laney didn't have a comeback. Couldn't even manage a glare for taking a swipe at her when she'd been dealt such a hard blow. But then the swipe only confirmed for her exactly what kind of person Emerson was. Not the sterling, upstanding DA of Longview Ridge. A man who was capable of striking out like that could be capable of doing other things, too. Like cheating on his wife. Of course, it was a huge leap to go from that to murder, but Laney wasn't taking him off her very short suspect list.

"Emerson," Owen said, no anger in his voice, though there seemed to be a low warning, "come back tomorrow and I'll take your statement."

Owen got a slight jab, too, when Emerson flicked him an annoyed glance. However, the man finally turned and walked out. Kellan looked at Emerson. Then at Owen. Finally at her.

She had no idea what Kellan was thinking, but something passed between him and Owen. One of those unspoken conversations that siblings could have. Or rather, she supposed that was what it was.

She'd never quite managed to have a relationship like that with Hadley.

"SAPD will want to talk to Laney tomorrow," Kellan said to Owen. He checked his watch. "But it's late. Why don't you go ahead and take Laney to the ranch so you two can try to get some rest?"

Laney practically jumped to her feet. "No. I can't go there. It could put Addie in danger."

"We're taking precautions," Kellan assured her. "And I didn't say to take you to Owen's but rather the ranch. You can't go back to Owen's place because the CSIs are there processing the scene, but our grandparents' house is in the center of the property. No one lives there on a regular basis, so it's been kept up for company, seasonal ranch hands and such. Plus, it has a good security system. Addie, Francine, Gunnar and Jack are headed there now."

Jack was Kellan and Owen's brother. And he was also a marshal. Another lawman. But that didn't mean Laney could trust him.

"What about your fiancée?" she asked Kellan. Laney knew her name was Gemma, and she'd met her several times. "She shouldn't be alone at your place."

"She won't be. She'll be going to my grandparents' house, too. Eli's taking her there."

Eli was yet another brother and a Texas Ranger. So, she would be surrounded by Slater lawmen. Not exactly a comforting thought, but it could be worse.

As Addie's uncles, they'd do whatever it took to protect the baby.

"I'll have two reserve deputies drive Owen and
you, and once Eli and Jack are in place at the ranch,
I can have them come back here to help with the investigation," Kellan told them. "With Owen at our
grandparents' house, Addie won't have to be away
from her dad."

Until he'd added that last part, Laney had been
ready to outright refuse. She hadn't wanted to do
anything to put the child in more danger, or to separate father from child. Still, this was dangerous.

"There's a gunman at large," she reminded him.
"If he comes after me again, I shouldn't be anywhere
near Addie, Gemma or Francine."

Owen stared at her a moment. "Whoever sent that
gunman could try to use Addie to get to you. They
would have seen the way you reacted, the way you
tried to protect her. They would know she's your
weak spot."

Addie was indeed that. It had crushed Laney to
think of the baby being hurt.

Owen dragged in a weary breath before he continued, "It'll be easier to protect you both at the same
time, and it'll tie up fewer resources for Kellan. He
needs all the help he can get here in the office to
work the investigation and try to get a confession
out of Rohan Gilley."

She mentally went through what he was saying

and hated that it made sense. Hated even more that she didn't have a reasonable counterargument. She was exhausted, and it felt as if someone had clamped a fist around her heart. Still, Laney didn't want to do anything else to hurt Owen's precious little girl.

"I'm a PI," Laney reminded Owen. Reminded herself, too. "I can arrange for my own security. I'll be okay."

She saw the anger flash in Owen's eyes, which were the color of a fierce storm cloud. "I don't need to remind you that your assistant is dead. Or that you're in danger. So I'd rather you not add to this miserable night by lying to yourself. Or to me—*again*. When it comes to me, you've already met your quota of lies."

This was more than a swipe like the one Emerson had given her. Much more. Not just because it was true but especially because it was coming from Owen. It drained what little fight she had left in her and that was why Laney didn't argue any more when Owen gathered up his things and led her out the front door to a waiting cruiser.

Obviously, Kellan and Owen had been certain they could talk her into this. Which they had.

"This is Manuel Garcia and Amos Turner, the reserve deputies," Owen said when he hurried Laney into the back seat with him. The deputies were in the front.

Laney recognized both of them. That was because

whenever she was in town or dealing with the other ranchers, she'd kept her eyes and ears open. For all the good it'd done. Owen's ranch had been attacked, Joe was dead and she was no closer to the truth than she had been when she'd lied her way into getting a job with Owen.

It would have been so easy to slip right into the grief, fear and regret. The trifecta of raw emotions was like a perfect storm closing in on her. But giving in to it would only lead to tears and a pity party, neither of which would help.

"I'm sorry," she said to Owen. That might not help, either, but she had to start somewhere. "Believe me when I say I didn't mean for any of this to happen."

The interior of the cruiser was dimly lit, yet she could clearly see Owen's eyes when he looked at her. Still storm gray. It was a different kind of intensity than what was usually there. When he'd looked at her before—before he'd known who she was and the lies she'd told him—there'd been…well, heat. Though he might not admit it, she'd certainly seen it.

And felt it.

Laney had dismissed it. Or rather she had just accepted it. After all, Owen was from the superior Slater gene pool, and the DNA had given him a face that hadn't skimped on the good looks. The thick black hair, those piercing eyes, that mouth that looked capable of doing many pleasurable things.

She dismissed those looks again now and silently cursed herself for allowing them to even play into this. She had no right to see him as anything but a former boss who had zero trust in her. Maybe if she mentally repeated that enough, her body would start to accept it.

"Believe me when I say I'm sorry," she repeated in a whisper, forcing her attention away from him and to the window.

Some long moments crawled by before he said anything. "You were close to your assistant, Joe Henshaw?"

The question threw her. Of course, she hadn't forgotten about Joe, but she'd figured that learning more about the man hadn't been on the top of Owen's to-do list. Plus, he hadn't even mentioned whether or not he would start to accept her apology.

"We were close enough, I suppose," she answered. "He worked for me about a year, and I trusted him to do the jobs I assigned him to do."

"Did he ever come to my ranch?" Owen fired back as soon as she'd answered.

Oh, she got it then. Laney knew the reason he'd brought up the subject. He wanted to measure the depth of her lies. "No. I only had phone contact with Joe when I worked for you. I didn't bring anyone to the ranch," she added.

From his reflection in the mirror, she could see that he was staring at her as if waiting for her to say more. Exactly what, she didn't know. When she turned back to him, Laney still didn't have a clue.

"I just want to know who and what I'm dealing with," Owen clarified. "Joe was your lover?"

"No." She couldn't say that fast enough and shook her head, not able to connect the dots on this one. "He worked for me, *period*."

Now it was Owen who looked away. "Just wanted to make sure I wasn't dealing with something more personal here."

"You mean like a lover's spat gone wrong," she muttered. The fact he had even considered that twisted away at her almost as much as the regret over lying to him.

"No. Like Terrance McCoy killing your assistant as a way of getting back at you."

Everything inside Laney stilled. Only for a moment, though. Before the chill came again. Mercy. She hadn't even considered that. But she should have. She was so tied up in knots over Emerson having killed Hadley that she hadn't looked at this through a cop's eyes. Something she'd always prided herself on being able to do. She'd never quite managed it with Hadley, though.

"Hadley's my blind spot." Laney groaned softly and pushed her hair away from her face.

She steeled herself to have Owen jump down her throat about that, to give her a lecture about loss of objectivity and such. But he didn't say anything.

Laney waited, staring at him. Or rather, staring at the back of his head because his attention was on the window.

"Addie's my blind spot," he said several long moments later. "I didn't want her in the middle of whatever this hell this is, but she's there."

Laney had to speak around the lump in her throat. "Because of me."

"No. Because of whoever hired those men to come to my house and go after you." He paused, turning so they were facing each other. Their gazes met. Held. "Don't ever lie to me again."

Not trusting her voice, Laney nodded and felt something settle between them. A truce. Not a complete one, but it was a start. If she was going to get to the bottom of what was going on, she needed Owen's help and, until a few seconds ago, she hadn't been sure she would get it.

The deputy took the turn off the main road to the Slater Ranch, which sprawled through a good chunk of the county. Kellan ran the main operation, just as six generations of his family had done, but Owen and his brothers Jack and Eli helped as well, along with running their own smaller ranches.

Separate but still family, all the way to the core.

It occurred to her that she might have to go up against all those Slater lawmen if it did indeed come down to pinning this on Emerson. But Laney was too exhausted to think about that particular battle right now.

"For the record," she said, "I told you the truth about most things. I grew up with horses, so I know how to train them. And every minute I spent with Addie—that was genuine. I enjoyed being with her. Francine, too," she added because the part about Addie sounded...personal.

A muscle flickered in Owen's jaw. "What about the day in the barn?" He immediately cursed and waved that off.

When he turned back to the window, she knew the subject was off-limits, but it wasn't out of mind. Not out of her mind anyway. And she did not need him to clarify which barn, which day. It'd been about a month earlier after he'd just finished riding his favorite gelding, Alamo. Owen had been tired and sweaty, and he'd peeled off his shirt to wash off with the hose. She'd walked in on him just as the water had been sluicing down his bare chest.

Laney had frozen. Then her mouth had gone dry.

Owen had looked at her and it had seemed as if time had stopped. It had been the only thing that had stopped, though. Laney had always known her boss was a hot cowboy, but she'd gotten a full dose of it that day. A kicked-up pulse. That slide of heat through her body.

The physical need she felt for him.

She hadn't done a good job of hiding it, either.

Laney had seen it on his face and, for just a second—before he'd been able to rein it in—she had seen the same thing in Owen's eyes.

Neither had said anything. Laney had calmly dropped off the saddle she'd been carrying and walked out. But she'd known that if she hadn't been lying to him, that if they'd been sitting here now, with no secrets between them, she would have gone to him. She would have welcomed the body-to-body contact when he pulled her into his arms. And she would have let Owen have her.

Owen knew that, too.

Just as they had done that day in the barn, their gazes connected now. They didn't speak, and his attention shifted away from her just as his phone dinged with a text message.

"Jack's got Francine and Addie all settled in," Owen relayed. He showed her the picture that his brother had included with the text. It was of Addie, who was sound asleep.

Laney smiled. Addie looked so peaceful and, while it didn't lessen her guilt over the attack, at least the little girl didn't seem to be showing any signs of stress.

Laney was still smiling when she looked up at Owen and realized he had noticed her reaction. And perhaps didn't approve.

Despite that shared "barn memory" moment, he probably didn't want her feeling close to his daughter.

Laney certainly couldn't blame him. She was about to bring up the subject again about her making other arrangements for a place to stay, but Owen's phone rang.

It was Kellan and, while Owen didn't put the call on speaker, it was easy for Laney to hear the sheriff's voice in an otherwise quiet cruiser.

"Just got a call from the CSI out at your place," Kellan said. "They found something."

Chapter Five

A listening device.

That was what the CSIs had found in the bedroom of the guesthouse where Laney had been living. Owen figured the thug who'd broken in had planted it there, but that didn't tell him why. What had those men been after? What had been so important for them to hear that they'd been willing to risk not only a break-in but also a shoot-out with a cop?

It was those questions and more that had raced through his mind half the night.

The other half he'd spent worrying if he'd done the right thing by bringing Laney here to his grandparents' old house. He needed to talk to Kellan about other options, but he figured his brother was getting some much-needed sleep right now. Owen hoped he was anyway, since Kellan had opted to stay the night at the sheriff's office.

Owen got out of the bed he'd positioned right next to Addie's crib—one they had borrowed from

Francine's friend. Addie was still sacked out, thank goodness, and since it was only 5:00 a.m., she should stay that way for a while. Just in case she woke up, though, he took the baby monitor with him into the adjoining bathroom. Francine had a monitor, too, and she was right across the hall, bunking with Laney in the master bedroom. Gemma was in the only other bedroom upstairs.

Owen grabbed a quick shower, dressed and headed downstairs to make coffee, but someone had already beat him to it. Someone had obviously beat him to getting up, too, because Eli and Jack were at the kitchen table, drinking coffee. They looked as if they'd been at it for a while.

"Get your beauty sleep?" Eli asked. His voice was like a grumbling drawl, and Owen figured the comment was just his way of showing brotherly "affection." Eli showed it a lot.

Owen had never been able to tell if Eli was truly just a badass or if he'd just been in a sour mood for the past decade. Either way, he appreciated him being here. The nice thing was, he didn't even have to say it. This was the sort of thing that family did for each other.

"The question should be—did our little brother get his beauty sleep *alone*?" Jack smiled as he gulped down more coffee.

Owen shot him a scowl, not completely made up

of brotherly affection because he didn't like even joking about this. "I'm not having sex with Laney."

Both Eli and Jack raised eyebrows, causing Owen to curse and repeat the denial.

"Maybe you didn't last night..." Jack took his life into his own hands by continuing to smile.

"Never," Owen insisted, pouring himself some coffee as if he'd gone to battle with it. "Laney works for me—*worked* for me," he corrected. "And I shouldn't have to remind you that she lied to me about who she was."

"Yeah, but you didn't know about the lie until last night." Jack again. "There were plenty of nights before that when sex could have happened. Laney's a looker."

She was, and before he could rein it in, Owen got a flash of that look she'd had on her face when she'd seen him in the barn. There'd been a whole lot of lust in the air in that moment.

"Hard to believe you wouldn't go after her," Jack commented.

Owen's scowl got a whole lot worse. "Are you looking to get your butt busted before the sun even comes up?"

Of course, Jack smiled.

Eli shrugged and kept his attention on his coffee. "Well, then, if you're not interested in Laney, then maybe I'll ask her out."

Owen hadn't thought his scowl could get worse,

but he'd been wrong. "Laney lied to me," Owen emphasized in case they'd both gone stupid and had forgotten. "And because she lied, I didn't know there was a possibility that thugs could come to my house."

Eli lifted his shoulder again. "Bet she didn't know it, either. Plus, she lied because she wants justice for her sister. A good cause even if she didn't go about it the right way." He paused. "She's taken some hard hits, and she's still standing. Sounds like my kind of woman." He gave a satisfied nod. "Yeah, I'll ask her out."

Owen felt the snap of anger as he caught Eli's arm, ready to drag him out of the chair. The fact that Jack kept smiling and Eli didn't punch him for the grab clued Owen into the fact that this had been some kind of test. A bad one.

"Told you Owen was attracted to her," Jack said with a smirk.

Yeah, a test, all right.

Eli shook off Owen's grip the same easy way he shrugged, took out his wallet and handed Jack a twenty. So, not just a test but also a bet. One involving his sex life.

Owen was about to return verbal fire, but the sound of footsteps stopped him, and a moment later Laney appeared in the doorway. She immediately froze, her gaze sliding over his brothers before it settled on him.

"Did something else happen? Is something

wrong?" The words rushed out and alarm went through her eyes.

"No," Owen assured her. Nothing wrong other than him wanting to throttle his brothers.

Laney released the breath she'd obviously been holding and put the laptop she'd tucked beneath her arm on the table. "Good. That's good." She fluttered her fingers to the stairs. "Addie's still asleep, but Francine and Gemma are in there. Gemma wants to hold her when she wakes up."

Owen had suspected as much. His little girl would get lots of attention today. Too bad it was because of the attack. Addie had been in danger, and it was going to be a very long time before he or anyone else in his family got past that.

Laney looked at his brothers again, probably thinking she'd interrupted a sensitive conversation about the investigation. She hadn't, and there was no way in hell he'd tell her about the bet. But it was time for him to get his focus back where it belonged. Better to deal with the investigation than to notice the fit of the jeans Laney had borrowed from Gemma.

"The Ranger lab has the eavesdropping device," Owen said, turning to get her a mug from the cupboard. "They might be able to find where the info was being sent."

That eased some the alarm on her face, and she poured herself some coffee. "The audio was being sent to a receiver or computer?"

"It looks that way." And since he'd started this briefing, Owen added, "Terrance is coming in this morning."

"Terrance," she repeated, her voice strained. "I want to be there when you question him."

Owen shook his head. "I can't allow you in the interview room—"

"I can watch from the observation room." She paused, met his gaze. "I just want to hear what he has to say."

He didn't have to think too hard on this. Owen had to take Laney in to make a statement, so she'd already be in the building when Terrance arrived. Since there was no harm in her observing, he nodded and then tipped his head to the laptop. It, too, was a loaner from Gemma.

"Have you been able to access copies of the info you had stored on your computer?" he asked.

"Not yet. But I will. I've been going through Joe's files on our storage cloud."

Owen immediately saw the shimmer in her eyes. Not alarm this time. She was fighting back tears.

"I need to find Joe's killer." Her voice was just above a whisper. "I need to put an end to this so your life can get back to normal."

He nearly laughed. It'd been so long since he'd had normal, Owen wasn't sure that he'd recognize it. First, losing Naomi and becoming a single dad, and then losing his father. Yes, it had been a while.

"I emailed both Kellan and you the link and password to the files," Laney said a moment later. "Joe was more tech savvy than I am, so I'm hoping he has hidden files. It's a long shot, but something might turn up."

"Gemma could maybe help you with that," Jack said. "Or I know someone else who might be willing to take a look. She's in WITSEC, but she's got good computer skills."

"Caroline Moser," Laney provided.

Owen hadn't been sure that Laney would know who Jack was talking about, but Longview Ridge was a small town with lots of gossip. Plenty of people knew that Caroline and Jack had been lovers. In love, Owen mentally corrected. But Caroline had been injured in an attack and couldn't remember any of that. Ditto for not remembering the crime she'd witnessed.

His father's murder.

When Caroline got her memory back, they'd know the truth. Well, maybe. It was possible that she hadn't even seen the killer. Obviously she had recalled how to work a computer, so that was a good sign. What they needed, though, were a lot of good signs, not just for his dad's killer but also for the attack at his place.

"Don't involve Caroline in this just yet," Owen advised Jack. He wanted Caroline to concentrate on recovering so they could get those answers about his father even sooner.

Jack nodded in a suit-yourself gesture. "What about the gunman you have in custody? Rohan Gilley. He couldn't have killed Laney's assistant because he was in jail at the time, but maybe we can use the murder to twist him up a little? Maybe let him believe his boss is tying up loose ends and he could be next?"

It was a good angle, and Owen would definitely try it and others. It riled him that he might have to offer Gilley some kind of plea deal, but that might be the fastest way to put an end to whatever this was.

And that brought Owen to the next part of this conversation. A part that neither of his brothers was going to like. Neither did he, but it was something they needed to know.

"About a week ago, I asked a PI out of Austin to take a look at the file on Dad's murder," Owen started. "I just wanted someone with a fresh eye."

That definitely got Eli and Jack's attention. Laney's, too. "I'm guessing the PI didn't find anything or you would have told us," Jack remarked.

"You're right. But I have to consider that Dad's killer might have found out and decided a *fresh look* wasn't a good idea, that it would lead us to him or her."

Since his brothers didn't seem the least bit surprised by that, Owen knew they had already considered it.

"I do new runs on the info all the time," Eli commented. "Calls, going out to the crime scene, and

I'm not quiet about it. It seems to me that if the killer was keeping tabs on us, he would have come after me. I'd be the easiest one to get to."

He would be. Unlike Jack, Kellan and him, Eli didn't have any full-time help on his place, only a couple of part-time hands who checked on his horses when he was working.

"I do runs, too," Jack interjected, "and if the killer came after one of us, I figure it'd be me. Because I'm the smartest," he added, no doubt to lighten the mood.

It didn't work, but then nothing could when it came to the hell they'd been through for the past year.

Owen finished off his coffee and put the cup in the dishwasher. "I'll go up and check on Addie." He looked at Laney. "Then I'll call the reserve deputies to escort us to the sheriff's office so I can get ready for Terrance's interview. You can give your statement while we're waiting for him."

Owen headed for the stairs, but he only made it a few steps before his phone rang, and he saw Kellan's name on the screen. The call got his brothers and Laney's attention, because they all looked at him. Waiting.

Since this could be an update on the investigation, he went ahead and put it on speaker.

"Eli, Jack and Laney are here," Owen said in greeting to let Kellan know their conversation wouldn't be private.

Kellan didn't hesitate. "The lab just called and they found where the info from the eavesdropping device was being sent." Kellan paused and cursed softly. "You should come on in so we can discuss how to handle this."

Owen silently groaned. If Terrance was behind this, then Kellan would have quickly volunteered that information. "Did Emerson set the bug?" Owen came out and asked.

"No." Kellan paused again. "But according to the crime lab, his wife did."

NETTIE KEATON.

The woman's name just kept going through Laney's head while she drove with Owen and the reserve deputies to the sheriff's office. And there were questions that kept repeating, too.

Why had Nettie done something like this? Had the woman also been responsible for the attack?

Not only was Nettie the DA's wife, she was also Owen's sister-in-law. Family. From all accounts, Nettie had been there for Owen after he'd lost his wife and had even taken care of Addie until Owen had been able to find a nanny. It was an understatement that their tight relationship wouldn't make the interview with her pleasant. But Laney hoped that it would be objective, that Owen would dig hard to get to the truth.

"The CSIs didn't find dust on the listening device," Owen said, reading from the report that Kellan had messaged him just as they were leaving the house. "But since it'd been planted beneath the center drawer of your desk, it's possible dust wouldn't have had time to accumulate on it."

In other words, there was no way to pinpoint how long it had been there. It turned Laney's stomach to think that maybe it had possibly been there for weeks. Or maybe even the entire time she'd worked for Owen. Of course, that only led to another question—had Nettie known who she was when she'd come to Longview Ridge?

Laney had already searched back through her memory to try to figure out if her sister had ever mentioned meeting Nettie. She didn't think so, but Hadley hadn't told her everything.

"The audio feed from the listening device was going to a computer registered to Nettie," Owen noted.

Yes, she'd already come to that conclusion from what Kellan had said earlier. "I'm assuming Kellan will get a search warrant for it?" she asked.

Owen looked up from the report and his eyes narrowed for just a moment. Then he glanced away as if frustrated. "Kellan and I aren't wearing blinders when it comes to Nettie. If she's done something wrong, we'll get to the bottom of it."

After just seeing his reaction, Laney didn't doubt that part, but there was another layer there. Some more fallout. Because this could add another family scar on top of plenty of other wounds.

"Emerson knew who you were," Owen said a moment later. "If Nettie did, too, then this could have been her way of keeping tabs on you. It doesn't make it right," he quickly added. "But if she was worried about you coming after Emerson, that could be her justification for doing it."

True, and Nettie wouldn't have had trouble getting into the guesthouse. Heck, she probably had a key. There'd been plenty of times when Laney had been in the pasture working with a horse and wouldn't have been near the guesthouse. Nettie could have easily gotten in without anyone noticing.

Owen's gaze came back to her. "Of course, you know I don't believe Nettie would put me or Addie in danger by sending those thugs to the ranch. And I just can't see her hiring a hitman to go after your assistant."

Laney gave that some thought and considered something else that Owen wasn't going to like. "Maybe she didn't think things would go that far. You were still at work, and she might have thought Francine would take Addie with her to the nursing home. She might have *justified* what she did by believing her niece wouldn't be in harm's way."

A muscle flickered in his jaw, but his eyes didn't narrow again. Nor did he dismiss what she was saying. That meant he'd likely already considered it. *Was considering it*, she amended. It wouldn't be easy for him, but he would do what was right. So would she. And maybe what they found wouldn't hurt him even more than he already had been.

The reserve deputy pulled to a stop in front of the sheriff's office. When they went inside, Laney steeled herself to face Nettie and Emerson, who would almost certainly be there with his wife. But they weren't in the waiting area.

However, Terrance was.

When he looked at her and smiled, Laney forced herself not to take a step back and kept her shoulders squared. That was hard to do. Even though she hated feeling it, Laney remembered the way he'd attacked her, that look in his eyes clearly letting her know he'd wanted to kill her.

Terrance was masking that look today. Maybe because he no longer hated her, or perhaps he'd just managed to rein it in. If so, Laney needed to do some restraining of her own. It was best not to show any signs of fear or weakness around a man like Terrance.

It was the first time she'd seen Terrance since she'd testified against him at his trial for assaulting her. That'd been six months ago and his short stint in jail hadn't changed him much. With his acne-scarred face and beaked nose, he was still a very unattractive man in an expensive suit.

Next to Terrance was another suit and someone else she recognized. The bald guy reading something on his phone was Terrance's lawyer. He, too, had been at the trial and had tried every dirty trick in the book to have his client declared not guilty. It hadn't worked, which was probably why the man gave her an unmistakable sneer.

"Laney," Terrance greeted her, getting to his feet. "Did I scare you?" That oily smile still bent his mouth a little.

"No." Laney made sure she looked him straight in the eyes. "Why should I be afraid of you? We both know if you touch me again, you'll spend a lot longer than six months in a cage."

Terrance's washed-out blue eyes dismissed her with a glance before he turned to Owen. "I'm guessing you must be Deputy Slater, the local yokel who ordered me here for an interview?"

"Deputy Slater," Owen confirmed, ignoring the insult as Terrance had ignored Laney's comment. Instead he looked at Kellan, who was stepping into the doorway of his office. "I was about to send our guests to an interview room where they can wait until you're ready to talk to them."

"We've already waited long enough," Terrance snapped.

"And you'll wait some more. Interview room." Owen pointed up the hall, his voice and body language an order for them to go there. "Since you're on probation, it probably wouldn't be a good idea for you not to cooperate with the cops. Even when they're local yokels," he added a heartbeat later.

Apparently, Owen hadn't ignored the insult after all, and it caused Laney to smile. Not for long, though. She spotted Nettie sitting in Kellan's office. Terrance, who looked in at the woman, too, as his lawyer and he walked past Kellan, cast a glance at Laney over his shoulder. She wasn't quite sure what to make of that look, but she dismissed it when Nettie jumped to her feet.

"You planted that bug so that I'd get blamed for it," Nettie immediately blurted. "Well, you won't get away with it. I won't have you telling lies about me."

Laney had already considered that Nettie might try to blame her for this, but it was odd that the woman was the one making the denial. Laney had thought it would come from Emerson first.

As she'd done with Terrance, Laney faced Nettie head-on. "I didn't plant a bug, didn't tell lies about you and I certainly didn't have men fire shots at Addie, Owen and me."

There was a bright fire of anger in Nettie's eyes as she glared at Laney before snapping at Owen. "Please tell me you don't believe her."

Owen dragged in a breath and put his hands on his hips. "I believe her. Laney could have been killed in that attack, so she's not the one who set this up."

Nettie opened her mouth, closed it and then made a sound of frustration that might or might not have been genuine.

"I have no motive to plant a bug and link it to you," Laney reminded the woman.

"But you're wrong about that. You do have a motive. This could be your way of getting back at Emerson."

That got Laney's attention and she stared at Nettie.

Nettie practically froze, but Laney could see the woman quickly gathering her composure. "I don't know exactly what grudge you have against my husband," Nettie amended, "but I believe that's why you're here. Why you came to Longview Ridge. Whatever it is you think about him, you're wrong. Emerson's a good man."

"Is he?" Laney challenged.

Nettie made a sound of outrage and turned to Kellan this time. "Can't you see that I'm being set up?" She flung a perfectly manicured finger at Laney. "And that she's the one who's trying to make me look guilty of something I didn't do."

Kellan dragged in his own long breath. "The eavesdropping device was linked to a computer registered to you. Before Owen and Laney came in, I told you that I needed to have the CSIs do a search of your house to find that computer—"

"No." Nettie practically shouted that and then, on

a groan, sank down into the chair next to Kellan's desk. "If you do that, then Emerson will know about these ridiculous allegations."

Owen and Laney exchanged glances. "Emerson doesn't know?" Owen asked, looking first at Nettie and then Kellan.

Kellan shook his head. "Nettie asked me to hold off telling him until she had a chance to clear this up."

"I don't want Emerson bothered by this nonsense," Nettie piped in.

"There's no way around that," Kellan assured her. "I have probable cause to get a search warrant, and I'll get it. The lab will go through all the computers in your home and, from the preliminary info gathered, there'll be a program to link to the eavesdropping device found in the guesthouse where Laney lives."

Laney braced herself for another onslaught of Nettie's temper, but the woman stayed quiet for a moment. "Someone must have broken into my house and added the program," Nettie finally said and then her gaze slashed back to Laney. "You did it. You broke in when I wasn't there so you could set me up."

Laney sighed and was about to repeat that she had no motive, but Owen spoke first. "Just let the CSIs look at the computers and we'll go from there. The techs will be able to tell when the program was installed, and if someone did that while you weren't there, then you might have an alibi."

Nettie didn't jump to agree to that and nibbled on her bottom lip for a few seconds. "Would Emerson have to know?"

Kellan groaned, scrubbed his hand over his face. "Yes. He's the DA, and even if he wasn't, this sort of thing would still get around."

Yes, it would get around, and then Emerson would likely hit the roof when he found out that CSIs were in his house looking for evidence against his wife. Laney was betting he'd accuse her just as Nettie had done.

"You're right," Nettie said several long moments later. Instead of nibbling on her bottom lip, it trembled. "Someone will tell him, but he'll know I don't have any reason to plant a bug. Emerson will be on my side. He won't believe I could do anything like this because I just wouldn't."

Laney didn't know Nettie that well, but it seemed as if the woman was trying to convince herself of Emerson's blind support. She decided to press that to see if it led to anything.

"Emerson's never mentioned me to you?" Laney asked.

Nettie's head whipped up. "What do you mean?" The anger had returned and had multiplied.

Laney decided to just stare at the woman and wait for her to answer. Kellan and Owen obviously decided to do the same, and their reaction brought Nettie back to her feet. However, the fiery eyes stayed firmly planted on Laney.

"I know you've told lies about my husband," Nettie said, her tone sharp, edgy. "I don't know the details, but I've heard talk. It's lies. All lies."

So, Emerson hadn't told his wife about his affair with Hadley. Of course, that probably wasn't something he'd wanted to discuss with her, especially since Emerson was claiming he was innocent.

Nettie hiked up her chin. "I suppose you want some kind of statement from me about that bug?" she asked Kellan.

He nodded. "And permission to search your house for the computers. If I don't get permission, then I'll have no choice but to get the warrant. Then plenty of people will know about this."

She squeezed her eyes shut, her mouth tightening as she took out her phone. "Let me call Emerson first." Nettie didn't wait for permission to do that. She walked out of the office, through the squad room and to the reception desk before she made her call.

Laney turned to Owen to get his take, but before she could say anything, she spotted Terrance again. He was outside the door of the interview room—where he could have heard the conversation they'd just had with Nettie.

"I don't owe you any favors," Terrance said to Laney, "but I'm going to do one for you anyway."

"What favor?" Laney didn't bother to tone down her very skeptical attitude.

Terrance gave her another of those slick smiles. "A couple of months before my trial, my legal team started gathering information that they thought would help with my defense. They hired PIs to follow you and people connected to you."

Laney's heart sped up. Hadley had been murdered just a month before Terrance's trial. Terrance had an airtight alibi for the murder—he'd been at a party and there were dozens of witnesses. But his PIs could have seen something.

"Did you know you were being followed?" Owen asked her.

Laney shook her head, her attention still fixed on Terrance. "You know who killed my sister?" She heard the quiver in her voice, felt the shudder slide through her body.

"No. But my lawyers were having Hadley followed. Not full-time but on and off to see if there was something they could use to prove my innocence."

"Cut to the chase," Owen demanded. "What the hell do you know about Laney's sister?"

Terrance smiled again when he tipped his head to Nettie. "Why don't you ask her?" He continued before any of them could attempt to answer, "The DA's wife was with Hadley the night she was murdered."

Chapter Six

Owen stared at Terrance, trying to figure out the angle as to why the man had just tossed them that lie. But there was nothing in Terrance's expression or body language to indicate that he was telling them anything but the truth.

Hell.

Was it actually true? Had Nettie not only known Hadley but also met with her?

Owen shifted his attention to Laney and noted that hers was a different kind of body language. A highly skeptical one. She huffed, folded her arms over her chest and stared at Terrance.

"Why would you volunteer that information to me?" Laney demanded.

It was a good starting point as questions went, but Owen had plenty of others for the man. And then he would need to confront Nettie if he felt there was any shred of truth to what Terrance had just said.

Terrance flashed the same smile he'd been doling

out since Laney and Owen had first laid eyes on the man in the sheriff's office. He was a slick snake, the type of man who assaulted a woman, and Owen had to rein in his temper because he wanted to punch that self-righteous smile off Terrance's smug face. That wasn't going to solve anything, though, and would make things a whole lot worse.

"I volunteered the info because I'm doing my civic duty," Terrance answered, and there was nothing sincere in his tone. "As Deputy Slater pointed out, I'm on probation. Withholding potential evidence could be interpreted as obstruction of justice. I wouldn't want that, because it could violate the terms of my parole."

Owen stepped closer and met Terrance eye to eye. "Yet if this so-called evidence is true, you withheld it for months."

Terrance lifted his hands palms up. "I've been in jail and I've been focusing my time and energy on… rehabilitation."

"My client didn't know the information was important," the lawyer added. When he took a step closer, as if he might come into Kellan's office, both Kellan and Owen gave him a warning glance that worked because he stayed put.

"It's true," Terrance agreed. "Until I overheard the conversation just a few minutes ago, I didn't make the connection between the DA's wife and Laney's dead sister." He turned to Laney then. "Here all this time, you thought your sister's killer was Emerson, and now I've put a cog in your wheel by handing you another suspect."

Laney continued to stare at him. "Two other suspects," she corrected. "You're high on my list of people who could have murdered Hadley."

She'd sounded strong when she said that, but Owen knew that, beneath the surface, this was eating away at her. After all, she was facing down the man who'd assaulted her and put her in the hospital.

"Do you have any proof whatsoever of what you're saying?" Owen demanded.

Terrance lifted his shoulder. "Reports from my PIs. It's possible they took photos, but if so, I don't remember seeing them."

Reports could be doctored. Photos could be, too. Still, Owen would need to treat this as any other potential evidence that fell into his lap. Because if Nettie was indeed connected to Hadley's murder, then she could have had something to do with the attack at his ranch.

That put a hard knot in his gut.

"I'll want everything from your PIs ASAP," Owen insisted.

Terrance nodded. "I'll get right on that. Wouldn't want it said that I didn't cooperate with the law." He glanced at Nettie, whose back was to them. She was pacing across the reception area while still on her phone. "And what about her? You think she'll cooperate?"

"She's not your concern," Kellan assured him, sounding very much like a sheriff who'd just given an order. "Come with me." He led Terrance and the lawyer into the interview room and shut the door before he came back to them.

"I didn't know Terrance was having me followed," Laney immediately volunteered. "I'm a PI, and I should have noticed something like that."

No way was Owen going to let her take the blame for this. "If Terrance didn't lie about the timing of this alleged meeting, you would have been in the hospital and then recovering from the injuries he gave you. A broken arm, three broken ribs and a concussion. That's a lot to distract you."

Laney quickly dodged his gaze while the muscles in her jaw tensed. Maybe she hadn't wanted him to dig into her medical records, but Owen considered it connected to the investigation of last night's attack. At least, that was what he'd told himself. After reading the police report of Terrance's assault, Owen now had to admit that it had become personal for him.

And that was definitely something he didn't want.

"I have no idea if Terrance is telling the truth about Hadley and Nettie," Laney went on a moment later. "Hadley never mentioned meeting Emerson's wife."

Owen had to consider that was because Hadley

had never gotten a chance to tell Laney. After all, Terrance had claimed his PIs saw the two women the same night Hadley had been murdered. That still didn't mean Nettie had killed her. Didn't mean that anything Terrance had told them was the truth.

Before Owen could talk to Kellan about how they should handle this, Nettie finished her call and came back toward them. "Emerson just left for a business meeting in Austin and will be gone most of the day," she said and then paused. "I didn't tell him about the eavesdropping device."

Owen only lifted an eyebrow, causing Nettie to huff, "You should have told him."

Nettie shook her head. "I know it's all some misunderstanding, that I had nothing to do with the eavesdropping device, so there's no reason to worry him." She turned to Kellan. "Go ahead and get someone in the house to take whatever you need. Just try to be finished with the search before Emerson comes home. Test the computers and have them in place so that he doesn't know."

No raised eyebrow for Kellan. Instead he gave Nettie a flat look. "I can't guarantee that. In fact, I'm pretty sure it'll take a couple of days to go through the computers once I get everything to the lab. You'll need to tell Emerson," he quickly added. "He'll hear it sooner or later, and I'll give you the chance to have him learn about it from you."

Nettie volleyed some glances between Kellan and

him as if she expected them to budge on their insistence that she tell her husband what was going on. They wouldn't. And Owen made certain that his expression let her know it. It didn't matter if this was all some kind of "misunderstanding." It still had to be investigated.

As did Terrance's accusations.

"If you want to interview Terrance, I can get a statement from Nettie," Owen offered his brother.

Nettie blinked, pulled back her shoulders. "A statement?" Her voice was sharp and stinging. "I've already told you I had nothing to do with that stupid bug."

"Why don't we take this to the second interview room?" Owen suggested, hoping this wouldn't escalate.

But it did.

Nettie didn't budge when Owen put his hand on her arm to get her moving. "A statement?" she repeated. Not a shout but close. She slung off Owen's grip and snapped at Laney. "You're responsible for this. You've somehow convinced them that I'm a criminal. I'm not. You're a liar, and now you're dragging me into those lies."

"Nettie," Kellan said, "you need to calm down and listen."

The woman ignored him and charged toward Laney. Nettie had already raised her hand as if to slap Laney, but both Laney and Owen snagged the woman by the wrist. The rage was all over Nettie's face now and she bucked against the restraint.

"I don't only need a statement about the bug," Owen snapped. "But also about your meeting with Hadley Odom."

Nettie's rage vanished. In its place came the shock. Only for a second, though. "I have no idea what you're talking about."

Because Owen was watching her so carefully, he saw something he didn't want to see. Nettie touched her hand to her mouth, then trailed it down to her throat. She did that while staring at him, her eyes hardly blinking. All signs that she was lying.

"You've never met Hadley Odom?" he pressed.

Her hand fluttered to the side of her face and she shook her head. "No. Why would I have met her? I don't even know who she is."

Kellan and Owen exchanged glances as Kellan stepped in front of Nettie. "What if I told you there could be proof that you not only knew this woman but that you met with her?"

Nettie huffed, "Then I'd say someone lied. Or that you're mistaken. I have to go," she added, tucking her purse beneath her arm. "Make those arrangements for the computers to be picked up. I need to go to Austin and talk to my husband."

Owen didn't stop Nettie when she walked out. She wasn't exactly a flight risk and, once they had more info on the computers—or from Terrance—

they could bring her back in for questioning. It'd
be necessary because Owen was certain that Nettie knew a lot more about this than she was saying.

Nettie paused when she reached the door and
glanced at them from over her shoulder. "Emerson's
going to ruin both of you when he finds out how
you've treated me," she declared just seconds before
she made her exit.

Owen kept his eyes on Nettie until she was out of
sight, then turned to get Kellan's take on what had
just happened. But he noticed Laney first. She was
pale and looking a little shaky.

"Nettie could have killed my sister," Laney said,
sinking down into the nearest chair.

Owen wanted to curse. He'd been all cop when
he'd been listening to Nettie and hadn't remembered
that this was more than a murder investigation to
Laney. She'd lost a member of her family, and he
knew what that was like. Knew that it could cut to
the core. It would continue to cut until Laney learned
the truth and found justice for her.

He knew plenty about that, as well.

"I'll take the interview with Terrance," Kellan
advised.

Still looking shaky, Laney got up. "I want to listen to what he has to say."

Judging from the way Kellan's forehead bunched
up, he was likely debating if that was a good idea.

But he finally nodded. "Take her to the observation room," he told Owen.

Owen did, but that was only because he knew he wouldn't be able to talk Laney out of it. Besides, she knew Terrance, and she might have some insight into whatever he said. Owen was betting, though, that Terrance wouldn't reveal anything incriminating. No way would he risk going back to jail, unless he was stupid.

And he definitely didn't strike Owen as stupid.

Just the opposite. Terrance could have told them about Nettie and Hadley's meeting as a way of covering himself. By casting doubt on Nettie, Terrance might believe it would take the spotlight off him when it came to Hadley's murder. It didn't. He had motive and means. As for opportunity… Yes, he had an alibi, but he could have hired someone to do the job.

Laney's top suspect in her sister's murder was Emerson. Or at least it had been before Terrance had just thrown Nettie into the mix. But Owen was going to take a hard look at Terrance himself.

"Are you all right?" Owen asked Laney when they stepped into the observation room. It was a small space, not much bigger than a closet, and it put them elbow to elbow.

"I will be," she answered after a long pause. That meant she wasn't all right at the moment. Of course, he hadn't expected her to absorb it all and look at this through a PI's eyes. Not when there was this much emotion at stake.

She kept her attention on the two-way glass window where Kellan, Terrance and his lawyer were filing into interview room. "I'll be better if I can figure out a way to put him back in a cage."

Owen made a sound of agreement and because he could feel the tight muscles in her arms, he put his hand on her back and gave her a gentle pat. That took her gaze off Terrance. She looked at him. Then she groaned.

"You're feeling sorry for me." She said it like an accusation. There was some anger in her eyes and her voice. "You're thinking about the way Terrance beat me up and how that's weighing on me—"

Owen didn't let her finish. He snapped Laney to him and kissed her. What she'd said was true, but for some reason, her anger riled him. It had obviously made him stupid, too, because his go-to response had been a hard kiss. That didn't stay hard. The moment his mouth landed on hers, everything changed.

Everything.

The anger melted away from him, along with the rest of his common sense, and in its place came the heat. Of course, the heat had been stirring for a while now between them, but the temperature inside him soared to scalding temps when he tasted her.

Oh, man.

He was toast. That taste and the feel of her in his

arms worked against him when she moved right into the kiss. Apparently she'd gotten rid of her anger, too, because she certainly wasn't fighting him. In fact, he was reasonably sure Laney was also feeling plenty of the heat.

The memories of that look in the barn slammed into him, mixing with this fresh fire and making this so much more than just a mere kiss. That, of course, only made him even more stupid. He shouldn't be lusting after her. Not with the chaos that was in their lives. And he darn sure shouldn't be wondering if he could take this kiss and let it lead them straight to bed.

She slid her arms around him, first one and then the other. Not some tight grip that would anchor him in place, which made it all the more dangerous. Because he suddenly wanted the anchor. He *ached* for it. Owen wanted to feel every inch of her against him. He silently cursed himself. And he cursed her, too.

When Owen heard Kellan's voice, he automatically tore himself away from Laney. It took him a moment to realize his brother wasn't in the observation room with them but that his voice was coming from the intercom. Kellan wasn't speaking to Laney and him, either. He was reading Terrance his rights.

Great. He'd gotten so tied up in that kiss and in the thoughts of bedding Laney, he'd forgotten there was something very important going on just one room over. They were there to hear what Terrance had to say, to try to look for any flaws or inconsistencies in his statement. Not for a make-out session. Even if that session had been damn good.

"Don't you dare apologize to me for that," Laney warned him. She ran her tongue over her bottom lip, causing his body to clench and then beg him to go back for more.

Owen stayed firmly planted where he was, though it was still plenty close to Laney. "I'm sorry that I lost focus," he settled for saying. "Not as sorry as I should be about the kiss."

It was the truth, but it was also true that it would happen again. That was why Owen groaned and cursed. He didn't need this kind of distraction, not with so much at stake, but his body didn't seem to be giving him a choice.

"We should have done something about this in the barn that day," he grumbled. "Then we would have burned it out of our systems by now."

At best, that was wishful thinking, but Laney didn't dismiss it. That told him she believed this was just lust, nothing more. But maybe that, too, was wishful thinking.

She smiled, but then quickly tightened her mouth to stop it. "I still have dreams about that day in the barn," she said.

Great. Now that was in his head. Dreaming about him having sex with her. Or rather, him wanting to have sex with her. The urge to do just that had been plenty strong that day. Still was. And Owen figured he'd be having his own dreams about not only that but the scalding kiss they'd just shared.

Thankfully, Kellan got their minds back on track when he sat across from Terrance at the table and opened with his first question.

"Where were you last night?"

The lawyer immediately took a piece of paper from his briefcase and handed it to Kellan. "We anticipated that you'd want to know that, so there's my client's alibi. As you can see, he was having dinner with several friends. I've included their names and contact information should you want to verify."

Slick move, Owen thought, and he had no doubts that the alibi would check out. That didn't mean Terrance hadn't been involved, though. Nope. He could have hired those men to break in. Heck, he could have hired them to plant the bug and set up Nettie.

Kellan looked over the paper the lawyer had given him. "Did you have a PI tail on Joe Henshaw, too?" he asked Terrance.

"Not recently, but yes, before my trial I did," Terrance admitted. "I've already told you that I had Laney and anyone connected to her under watchful eyes in case something turned up that I could use in my defense."

"You do know that Joe was murdered last night?" Kellan threw it out there.

Terrance nodded. "But I didn't see him, if that's

what you're about to ask next." He tipped his head to the paper. "And that proves I was elsewhere when he died."

Kellan didn't even pause. "You'd be willing to turn over your finances so I can verify that you didn't hire someone to kill him and hire others to attack Laney and kill Joe?"

Terrance smiled, definitely not from humor, though. It was more of amusement, and then he waved off whatever his lawyer had been about to say. "I'll turn them over to you if and when you get a warrant. I'm guessing, though, you don't have enough probable cause to do that, or you would have already gotten it."

"You're right. I don't have probable cause, not yet, but it's still early," Kellan answered. "A lot of hours left in the day, and I don't think it'd take much to convince a judge that I need a look at your financials. Not with your criminal record. Judges are a lot more apt to help when a convicted felon's name comes up in a murder investigation."

The anger flared in Terrance's eyes. Heck, his nostrils did, too, and that caused Owen to smile. It was nice to see Terrance get a little comeuppance, but it wasn't enough. They needed to get into his bank account, and despite what Kellan had just threatened, it might not happen. Terrance's lawyer would almost certainly stonewall any attempts at a warrant.

"How much did the woman he met online steal from Terrance?" Owen asked Laney.

"According to Terrance and the lawsuit he filed against me, it was about three million."

Owen's mouth fell open for a moment. "Damn."

Laney made a sound of agreement and glanced up at him. "A judge threw out his lawsuit, but from what I could gather, that three million was about two-thirds of Terrance's entire inheritance. His family wasn't happy about that."

No one other than the swindler would be happy about that. And with Terrance blaming Laney, it gave him three million motives to get back at her. Maybe even enough to kill or hire killers.

However, if Terrance had indeed paid someone to do his dirty work, his old-money background might have given him the skills to hide transactions like that. There could be offshore accounts. Heck, the funds could have come from a safe with lots of cash. Still, Owen would press to get that warrant. Right now, it was one of the few strings they had to tug on Terrance. If they tugged hard enough, things were bound to unravel and get them the proof they needed for an arrest.

"I've heard you have one of the so-called gunmen in custody," Terrance went on a moment later. "I gather he hasn't said anything about me hiring him, or you would have used that to arrest me."

There was enough snark in Terrance's tone to let

them know it was a challenge of sorts. No, the gunman hadn't pointed the finger at Terrance. Maybe he never would. But the longer they held the gunman, the higher the chance he might start to get desperate. The guy could ask for a plea deal in exchange for giving up his boss. Owen figured it would make plenty of people happy if it turned out to be Terrance.

Kellan stared at Terrance for several snail-crawling moments. "A lot of hours left in the day," he repeated. "Who knows what kind of dirt we'll be able to turn up on you."

This time Terrance flashed one of those cocky smiles, and Owen thought he saw some honest-to-goodness frustration slide into the man's eyes.

Terrance leaned forward, resting his forearms on the metal table. "Let me make your job easy for you, Sheriff Slater, because I want you to get off my back. I didn't hire any gunmen. I also didn't kill anyone, but I might have some more information that can put you on the right track."

Owen didn't miss the *more* and he found himself moving even closer to the glass. However, he also reminded himself that anything that came out of Terrance's mouth could be a lie or something meant to throw them off his track.

"I'm listening," Kellan said to the man.

Terrance opened a bottle of water first and had a long drink. "I've already told you that I hired PIs to follow people connected to my trial. That's how one of the PIs saw Nettie with Hadley." He paused. "But that wasn't the only time they saw Hadley."

That grabbed Owen's attention. Laney's, too, because she moved in closer, as well.

"I'll give you the reports from the PIs, of course," Terrance went on, "but I can tell you that about two days before Hadley was murdered, one of my men followed her to Austin."

Austin was a city only about an hour from Longview Ridge. Owen glanced at Laney to see if that rang any bells as to why her sister would go there, but she just shook her head.

"Hadley had a package with her," Terrance continued a moment later. "She went into the First National Bank on St. Mary's Street, stayed inside about a half hour, and when she came out, she didn't have the package with her. I know I'm not a cop, but I figure what she left there is worth you checking out."

"The photos of Emerson and Hadley," Laney said, snapping her eyes toward him. "Owen, we have to go get them now."

Chapter Seven

Now didn't happen. Despite Laney's insistence, she and Owen still did not have the photos even after Terrance had given them the name and street address of the bank where his PIs had seen Hadley.

Laney tried not to be frustrated and impatient about that, but it was impossible not to feel those things. And more. The urgency clawed away at her. She was so close to the evidence she needed to nail down Hadley's killer. She knew that in her gut. But she was going to have to tamp down that urgency because of one simple fact.

There was no safe-deposit box in Hadley's name at the First National Bank in Austin.

That meant either Terrance had lied about it or Hadley had used an alias. Laney was betting it was the latter. Hadley had wanted to make sure Emerson couldn't get to those pictures because she'd seen them as some kind of insurance policy. Proof of an affair with a married man.

Hadley had likely believed that as a DA, Emerson could have used his contacts to do searches of banks. And maybe he had indeed managed to do just that. But Laney wasn't giving up hope yet.

She would *never* give up hope, even if her patience was wearing thin.

Laney was pacing across the living room floor of Owen's grandparents' house—something she'd been doing a lot since they're returned an hour earlier from the sheriff's office. She stopped when Owen came in. One look at his face and she knew he didn't have good news for her.

"We're having trouble getting the search warrant for the bank." He sounded as frustrated as she felt. "The judge wants more verification that Hadley actually had a box there, and we just don't have it."

She touched her hand to the chain around her neck. It now only had the dragonfly pendant. "The bank manager has the key."

"A key that may or may not belong to one of the boxes," Owen reminded her. It wasn't his first reminder, either.

She wanted to argue with him. But she couldn't. She'd found the key in Hadley's apartment shortly after she'd been murdered. Laney had no proof that it was the one for the safe-deposit box Hadley had told her about. But Laney believed that it was. She believed it with all her heart. Too bad the judge wouldn't take her gut feeling as more verification for the search warrant.

"Even if it is the right key," Owen went on, "the manager says the bank employees can't just test that key on the boxes to find the right one."

"So, we need either the name Hadley used to get the box or the box number," she said, talking more to herself than to Owen. Laney forced herself to think, to try to figure out where Hadley might have left information like that.

Owen nodded, but it wasn't a nod of total agreement. "If the bank gets the right box and opens it, the manager says he can't release the contents without proper authorization."

Laney knew that, of course. Kellan had already told her that when she'd given him the key. The key that he'd then passed along to the bank manager. It still didn't make it easier to swallow. Plus, there was the hope that if and when the box was opened, there might be enough inside to spur the manager to help them get that warrant. After all, the photos could confirm motive for Hadley's murder.

Could.

Again, it would take some convincing with a judge, but at least they'd have tangible evidence. Emerson might fall apart and confess everything when confronted with pictures of him and his lover. At a minimum, it might cause Owen to start doubting him so that he and Kellan would take a much harder look.

"What about the PI report from Terrance?" Laney asked, but then she immediately waved that off.

That wasn't *proof.* Far from it. Terrance was a convicted felon and probably still held a grudge against her. He could have given them this info to send them on some wild-goose chase. One that would take the spotlight off him. One that would put her in an extra frazzled frame of mind. If so, it was working because that was where she was right now.

"Kellan's bringing in the PI who claims he saw Hadley go into the bank," Owen told her. "If the PI will sign a sworn statement as to what he saw, we can go back to the judge."

It was a long shot, but Laney refused to believe it wouldn't work. They had to find that box and get into it.

Owen walked closer to her, but still kept some distance between them. Something he'd been doing since that kiss in the observation room. Despite Laney telling him not to apologize for it, she could tell he was sorry. And that he regretted it.

"The bank manager did agree to go through all the names to see if there were any red flags," Owen said several moments later. "Is there any alias you can think of that Hadley might have used?"

It was something Kellan had already asked her, and Laney had come up with zilch. However, she had given Kellan the full names of Hadley and her parents, their pets and even childhood friends in case her sister had used any one of those.

"What about the PI report of the meeting between Nettie and Hadley?" she asked. "Has Terrance sent that to Kellan yet?"

"He emailed it, and Kellan sent me a copy."

Laney huffed. She wasn't frustrated that Terrance had sent it but because she'd wanted to see it as soon as it arrived.

"You read the report," Owen said, obviously picking up on her frustration. "It's on my computer."

Upstairs and in his bedroom. Or, at least, that was where his laptop had been the last time she'd seen it. Upstairs was also where his brother Eli and Gemma were. Addie and Francine, too. And while Laney liked all of them, she'd wanted to give Owen some space to be with his daughter and the rest of his family.

Owen motioned for her to follow him as he headed for the stairs. She did. "The reason I wasn't jumping through hoops to tell you about the report Terrance sent is that there's nothing in it other than what he told us at the sheriff's office."

That wasn't a surprise, but it was an annoying disappointment that only added to her frustration. Still, there was no way Terrance would give them anything they could use against him, and the PI likely wouldn't have realized the importance of a meeting between the two women. Still, Laney wanted to read it, study it, because it could possibly have something they could use.

"There are probably other reports," she said as they walked up the stairs. "Ones that maybe Terrance is holding on to. He can maybe use them as bargaining chips if it comes down to that."

His quick nod let her know that Owen had already considered it. "Kellan will try to get a search warrant on Terrance, too."

It would be easier to get that than it would be to get one for the bank, but Laney was betting Terrance had covered his tracks and there'd be nothing to find. There would definitely be nothing on his personal computer since he wouldn't risk going back to jail.

When they made it to Owen's bedroom, she was surprised that it was empty, but she could hear the chatter next door in the master bedroom. Chatter that she was betting wouldn't stop Eli from keeping watch. He was just doing it from the upstairs window now instead of the downstairs one. Laney had thankfully seen no lapse in security, which would need to continue until they found the person responsible for the attack.

Too bad they weren't any closer to doing that.

Owen's laptop was on a small folding table in the corner and he pulled out the chair for her to sit. The report was already on the screen. She noted the date and time.

"Lee Kissner," Laney said, reading the PI's name

aloud. "I don't know him personally, but he has a good reputation."

"A good rep, but he was working for Terrance," Owen pointed out.

She nodded. Shrugged. "I sometimes took on slimeball clients who were trying to clear their names." Laney could see this from that side of things, but it didn't make her feel better that Terrance had had her sister and her followed.

Laney read through the report, noting the description of the clothes Hadley was wearing. Red dress with silver trim and silver heels. Her sister did indeed have an outfit like that. In fact, the details matched all the way to the purse.

"According to the notes, Hadley didn't talk to anyone before going into the bank," Laney pointed out. "But someone—an employee—inside would have spoken with her. I'm assuming they've all been questioned?"

Owen nodded again. "One of the clerks thinks she might have remembered her when Kellan showed Hadley's photo. That's not enough to get a warrant," he quickly added. "The clerk isn't positive and doesn't remember why Hadley was there."

Laney groaned softly. She'd never been to that particular bank, but she'd checked the facts about it online, and it was huge. In addition, this visit would have happened months ago. That wasn't going to help, not with the steady stream of customers who would have gone in and out of there during that time.

As she continued reading, Laney could feel her frown deepening with each sentence. Her sister had spent a half hour inside the bank. That was plenty of time to not only open an account for a safe-deposit box but also enough time to lock the pictures inside and then come out.

Hadley hadn't spoken to anyone as she'd walked back to her car. She had simply driven away. The PI hadn't followed her since he was waiting on further instructions from Terrance. According to Lee Kissner, those instructions had been to suspend, at least temporarily, following Hadley. Too bad he hadn't stuck with her because it might have given them more clues about her killer.

Laney finished reading the report, stood and started to pace again, hoping that she could come up with an angle they could use to sway a judge. But nothing came to mind. Given the way Owen's forehead was furrowed, he was drawing a blank, too.

"I shouldn't have kissed you," he said. So, no blank after all. His mind hadn't been on the report, though she was certain he'd already given it plenty of thought.

"Yes," she agreed. "Loss of focus, blurred lines, bad timing." She'd hoped her light tone and dry smile would ease the tension on his face, but it didn't.

"Heat," he added to the list. But Owen didn't just say it. There was also some heat in his voice, along with a hefty dose of something Laney had been feeling all morning. Irritation and annoyance.

Owen looked at her the same moment she looked at him, and their gazes collided. Oh, mercy. Yes, there it was. So much fire. Way too much need. Way too much *everything*.

With all the memories going through her head, she wanted to smack herself as the image of Owen in the barn jumped right to the front of her mind. Followed by the more recent image of their kiss. Her body reacted and she felt that heat trickle through her.

"It's too dangerous for me not to be able to see all of this clearly," Owen added.

Until he'd said that, Laney had been about to go to him and kiss him. Nothing hard and deep like the one in the observation room. Just a peck to assure him that the heat could wait. It would have maybe sated her body a little, as well.

No assuring and sating now, though. They were just standing there, much too close, their gazes connected, the weight of the attraction and their situation bearing down on them.

It stunned her when Owen leaned in and brushed his mouth over hers. Stunned her even more that just a peck from him could dole out that kind of wallop.

It was a reminder that any kind of contact between them was only going to complicate things.

"Sorry to interrupt," someone said from the doorway.

Jack.

The man moved like a cat. And, despite the fact that he'd no doubt just witnessed that lip-lock, he didn't give his brother a ribbing smile.

"Just got a call from one of the hands," Jack told them. "Emerson's at your house, and he's demanding to see you."

Emerson had likely heard about Kellan taking the computers from his home. Or maybe Nettie had finally filled her husband in on everything.

"Emerson's already spoken to Kellan," Jack went on. "Guess he didn't get the answers he wanted, so he drove out to the ranch. I'm thinking it's not a good idea to have Emerson brought here."

"No, it's not," Owen agreed. He paused, his forehead bunching up even more. "Tell the hand to keep Emerson at my place. I'll drive over there to see him."

"Not without me—" Jack immediately said just as Laney piped in, "I want to see him, too—"

She knew Owen wasn't going to argue with his brother about going, but considered he would nix her request. He surprised her when he didn't. He gave her a nod.

"Just let me check on Addie first," Owen muttered.

Jack stepped to the side so that Owen could head there.

"No one in the room will bite," Jack added under his breath to her. "And if anyone can lighten the mood around here, it's Addie."

Jack was right. The little girl had a way of making everything better. Laney thanked him for the reminder and followed Owen, intending to stay in the hall and just get a glimpse of Addie. She didn't want to interfere with Owen's time with her. But Gemma remedied that as she took hold of Laney's arm and led her into the room.

Eli was in the exact spot that Laney thought he would be. Keeping watch at the window. Francine, seated near him, was sipping coffee. Laney smiled when she saw Addie on the bed, playing with a stash of stuffed animals, blocks and books. Addie smiled when she spotted her dad and put aside a toy horse to scoot toward him. Owen picked her up and kissed her cheek.

"Da-da," she said and dropped her head in the crook of his neck. The loving moment didn't last, though, when Addie's attention landed on Laney. "Aney," she attempted to say.

Laney didn't know who was more surprised when the little girl reached for her, but she felt a lot of relief. She'd been so afraid that Addie would associate her with the loud blasts from the gunfire and the terrifying run to the barn, but apparently she hadn't remembered that as well as she had Laney's name.

Owen passed Addie over to her, and when Laney had her in her arms, she had another surprise when Addie kissed her. The little girl babbled something that Laney didn't understand, but she caught the word *horsey*, so maybe she was talking about her toy stash.

Jack stepped up to Eli, probably to tell him about Emerson's arrival. When Jack went back into the hall, clearly waiting, that was Owen's cue to get moving.

Owen took Addie from Laney, giving his daughter another kiss before putting her back on the bed.

"My advice?" Eli said. "Put on a flak jacket because Emerson won't be a happy camper."

No, he wouldn't be, Laney thought. And it was possible that Nettie hadn't even told him the whole truth. The woman certainly would have put her own slant on things, and that, in turn, could cause Emerson to aim even more venom at Owen and her.

With Eli following them, Jack, Owen and Laney went back downstairs, and she heard Eli reset the security system as soon as they were out the door. They hurried into the cruiser so they wouldn't be out in the open too long. Of course, even a minute was probably too long as far as Owen as concerned.

Laney waited for Owen to remind her that it was an unnecessary risk for her to insist on going to this meeting. But he didn't. Maybe because he knew it wouldn't do any good. Besides, just seeing her might trigger Emerson into a fit of temper that could get him to spill the secret he'd been keeping about Hadley.

When Owen's house came into view, she immediately saw the crime scene tape fluttering in the breeze. Laney also noticed the sleek black car parked in front just a split second before she spotted Emerson. He was talking on his phone while he paced the front porch. And yes, he was riled. Every muscle in his body and face showed that. She had even more proof of the man's anger when they got out of the cruiser.

"What the hell do you think you're doing?" Emerson barked. The question wasn't aimed at Owen but rather at her.

"I'm trying to find out who nearly killed me and Owen," Laney answered. She didn't dodge Emerson's fiery gaze and definitely didn't back down. That was one of the few advantages of being just as riled as he was.

Despite the thick tension in the air, Owen somehow managed to stay calm as he unlocked the door. "There's a hired killer still at large, so we'll take this inside."

Emerson looked ready to argue, but he probably would have argued about anything at this point. He was spoiling for a fight.

Owen ushered her in first and Laney immediately saw that some of the items had been moved. Likely the CSIs' doing. She was betting the entire place had been checked for prints and trace evidence. An attack on a police officer's home would have caused everyone involved to be on the top of their game.

"You convinced Kellan to have a CSI go into my home," Emerson ranted at Laney as he came inside. He was still aiming his rage at her, too. "You upset my wife."

Owen didn't say anything until he had the door shut, and then he eased around to face his brother-in-law. "Nettie gave us permission to get the computers and have them analyzed. Did she tell you why?"

"Yes," Emerson snapped while Jack went to the living room window to keep watch. "It's because someone set her up so that it looks as if she planted a bug in your guesthouse." His narrowed eyes cut to Laney. "*You* set her up."

"I have no reason to do that." Laney tried to restrain her temper enough to keep her voice calm as well, but she wasn't quite as successful as Owen.

"Yes, you do, because you have some kind of vendetta against me." Emerson opened his mouth as if to say more, but then he closed it.

"What else did Nettie tell you?" Owen asked.

Silence. For a very long time. Emerson finally cursed under his breath and leaned against the wall. "Nettie said she met with her—" he tipped his head toward Laney to indicate the *her* "—sister." While there was still some anger in his voice, she thought she heard disgust, too.

"Hadley," Laney provided, though she was certain he knew her sister's name. "Hadley Odom," she said, spelling it out because she wanted to try to gauge his reaction.

Emerson dismissed her with a glance before his attention went back to Owen. "Nettie heard rumors that I was having an affair with *Hadley*." He said the name as if it were venom. "I'm guessing your sister started those rumors. So, Nettie confronted her. Apparently some private investigator witnessed the meeting and told Kellan about it."

"Did Nettie also confront *you* about the affair?" Owen asked.

Another long pause. "No. I didn't know that Nettie had heard those rumors until about two hours ago when she told me what's been going on."

"Rumors?" Owen questioned.

Since it sounded like the accusation that it was, Emerson cursed again. Then he groaned when Owen continued to stare at him. "I knew Hadley."

For only three words, they packed a huge punch. Finally, Laney had heard the man admit the truth. Truth about knowing her sister anyway. But she figured Owen was experiencing a gut punch of a different kind. As a cop, he wouldn't have wanted to hear his brother-in-law just confess to a relationship that was now a motive for murder.

Owen dragged his hand over his face and did some cursing of his own. "I need to read you your rights."

"I know my damn rights." Emerson pushed away from the wall. "I'm the damn DA!"

Owen went closer until they were toe-to-toe. "Then act like it and tell me what happened between Hadley and you. *Everything that happened,*" Owen emphasized.

Emerson's glare went on for so long that Laney thought he was going to clam up or demand that she leave. Maybe even ask for a lawyer. He didn't. He stepped back, shook his head. When his gaze returned to Owen, some of the anger was gone.

"I didn't kill her…" Emerson started. "I swear, I didn't kill her." He looked at Laney when he repeated that. "And I don't care what she told you. There was no affair. I barely knew her."

She studied his eyes, looking for any signs that was a lie, and Laney thought she detected one. However, she didn't know Emerson well enough to use his body language to try to convince Owen that the man wasn't being honest with them.

"How'd you meet Hadley?" Owen persisted when Emerson didn't continue.

"At a party that I attended in San Antonio. She came onto me, and I brushed her off. Told her I was

a married man, that I didn't play around on my wife."
Emerson glared at Laney as if challenging her to
prove him otherwise.

She couldn't.

She'd never personally seen the two of them together, but she'd believed her sister when Hadley
had told her about the affair. And, just as important,
she didn't believe Emerson. Yes, she could see Hadley coming onto him, but Hadley was a very attractive woman. She could have likely had her pick of
the men at that party and wouldn't have come onto
Emerson had he not been sending off the right sig-
nals. Or in this case, the wrong ones, since he was
a married man.

"I never saw Hadley again after that night," Emerson went on. "But she called me and claimed I'd
given her some kind of date rape drug at the party.
I denied it, but she didn't believe me. She cried and
carried on and told me that I'd be sorry."

Owen jumped right on that. "She threatened you?"

Emerson shook his head. "Not then, not with actual words anyway, but I knew she was very upset
and believed I'd actually drugged her. So upset that
when I first heard she was dead, I wondered if she'd
killed herself to set me up, to make it look as if I'd
murdered her. The woman was crazy," he added in
a mumble.

"Hadley didn't commit suicide," Laney insisted.
But she would give him a pass on the crazy part.

Hadley could be overly emotional. Still, Laney didn't believe she'd lied about having an affair with Emerson.

That meant Emerson was lying now.

"I agree about her not killing herself," Emerson said when Laney just kept glaring at him. "I realized that when I read the police report about her murder. The angle of the blunt-force trauma wound was all wrong for her to have done that to herself."

For just a moment Laney saw something more than anger. Maybe regret? Or it could be that Emerson had once had feelings for Hadley. That didn't mean, though, that he hadn't murdered her.

"There's more," Emerson continued, his gaze firing to Laney again. "And if you're responsible, so help me God, I'll make sure you're put behind bars."

Laney raised her hands. "What the heck are you talking about?"

"Blackmail." Emerson let that hang in the air.

Owen didn't even glance at her to see if she knew what Emerson meant, and that helped ease a little of the tension in her chest. Twenty-four hours earlier, if Emerson had accused her of something, Owen would have considered it a strong possibility. Or even the truth. But he now knew she wouldn't do anything like that.

"A couple of days ago, I got a phone call," Emerson explained. "The person used one of those voice scramblers, so I didn't know who it was. Still don't.

But the person claimed to know about the so-called affair I had with Hadley and threatened to tell Nettie if I didn't pay up. He said he had some kind of proof, but that's impossible. There's no proof because there was no affair."

Owen kept his attention nailed to Emerson. "You paid the blackmailer?" he snapped.

"No. Of course not. I'm not going to pay for something I didn't do. I put the person off, said that I needed time to get some money together. I've been using that time to try to figure out who's behind this."

Owen huffed and Laney knew why. Emerson's first response should have been to go to the cops. To his brother-in-law, Owen. Of course, that was the last thing a guilty man would have wanted to do.

"And did you find out who's behind this?" Owen challenged, the annoyance dripping off his tone.

Emerson shook his head, took out his phone. "I got another call yesterday. I recorded it and had a private lab analyze it. They were unable to get a voice match because of the scrambling device the person used, but the tech thought the caller was male. You can listen to the recording if you want."

Owen nodded.

Both Laney and Owen moved closer to Emerson's phone before the man hit the play button on his phone.

"I made it clear that I want thirty grand to keep

your dirty little secret," the caller said. "Since I don't have it yet, it's gonna cost you a whole lot more." The person rattled off a bank account number. "Fifty grand should do it. If I don't have the money in forty-eight hours, the amount doubles and then I go to your wife. I'll go to the press, too. Think of all the damage to your reputation when this comes out. You'll never be able to get the mud off your name."

Emerson clicked off the recording. "Don't bother tracing the bank," he said. "It's an offshore account."

That would indeed make it almost impossible to trace. But a conversation with the blackmailer might have given them plenty of clues. Laney so badly wanted to say that Emerson should have gone to Kellan and Owen with this, but she figured the man had already realized that.

"I won't send money," Emerson insisted. *"Can't,"* he amended. "Even if I had done something wrong, you know I don't have those kinds of funds. You know how little a DA makes in a small town. And I won't go to my wife's trust fund to pay a blackmailer to keep a secret that I don't even have."

Laney had known about Nettie's trust fund and that she was from a prominent family. It had come up when she'd run a background check on the woman. But Laney had assumed that Emerson had money of his own. Apparently not.

Emerson closed his eyes for a moment before he continued, "I don't want Nettie to know anything about this supposed affair. It'll upset her, and there's no reason for it."

Owen dragged in a breath. "Upsetting Nettie is only one part of this, and right now it's a small part. You withheld potential evidence in a murder investigation. That's obstruction of justice and you, of all people, should know that."

Laney figured that would bring on another wave of Emerson's rage, but it didn't come. The man merely nodded, as if surrendering. "I intend to talk to Kellan about that. In the meantime, I'll send you a copy of the recording from the blackmailer and will cooperate in any way the sheriff's office needs."

"Even financials?" Owen quickly asked.

Emerson didn't nod that time. He stared at Owen, and Laney wished she could see what was going on in his head. Obviously there was hesitation, but there seemed to be something more.

"Nettie and I don't have shared accounts," Emerson finally said. "That's the way it's written in her trust fund, that it can't become a joint account. I can give you access to mine but not hers."

"That'll do for now," Owen assured him.

Laney figured either Kellan or Owen would soon press Nettie to do the same.

Emerson made a sound to indicate that he would. "Just keep Nettie out of this, and I'll cooperate in any way that I can." He started for the door but then stopped when he reached Laney. "I didn't have an affair with your sister," he repeated.

She stood there and watched Emerson walk out. He drove away as soon as he got in his car, leaving Laney to try to sort through everything he'd just told them. That sorting, however, was getting some interference from her own emotions.

Emerson had stayed insistent about not having the affair, but he'd admitted to the obstruction of justice. Admitting to the first might cost him his marriage, but the second could put him behind bars. Why admit to one and not the other?

"You believe him?" Owen asked.

"If I do, it means my sister lied." She groaned softly, pushed her hair from her face. "Hadley could be irresponsible about some things, but lying about this wouldn't be like her." And Laney hated the words that were about to come out of her mouth. "Still, it's possible she did."

Owen nodded, not giving her his take on what he thought about all of it. But he was probably leaning in Emerson's direction. Specifically, leaning toward believing Emerson hadn't killed Hadley. After all, Owen didn't know Hadley, and it would make his personal life much easier if he didn't have to haul in his brother-in-law for murder.

He shut the door, took out his phone, and she saw him press Kellan's number. "I want to get that recording analyzed by the crime lab," he said. "And Kellan will need access to Emerson's phone records. We might be able to find out who made the two calls."

Maybe, but she figured a blackmailer would use a

burner cell, one that couldn't be traced. Especially if Terrance had been the one to make the calls. He was too smart to get caught doing something that stupid.

"Terrance knew about the meeting between Nettie and Hadley," she said while they waited for Kellan to answer. "The blackmail could be a way of his recouping some money he lost from his trust fund. It'll barely put a dent in what he lost, but he could be planning on going back to Emerson for more."

Owen made eye contact with her to let her know he was considering that, but he didn't get a chance to say anything because Kellan came on the line.

"I was just about to call you," Kellan volunteered. "We got a lucky break. The banker in Austin found the box. It's under an alias, Sandy Martell."

"How did they find out it belongs to Hadley?" Owen wanted to know.

"Because Hadley put Laney's name on it. There's a condition, though. Laney can only get into the box if she has the key. How convinced is Laney that the key she gave me is the one to the box?"

Good question, one that Owen had already asked Laney.

"I believe it is," Laney said. "I'm not positive, though."

Kellan stayed quiet for a moment. "All right. Then I'll meet you at the bank so I can give you back the key. Owen needs to get you there ASAP because the manager's going to let you have access."

Chapter Eight

A lot of thoughts went through Owen's mind, and not all of them were of relief.

Having Laney's name on the safe-deposit box meant it would eliminate hours and maybe days of red tape to not only locate the box but to gain them access to it. It also meant they might finally have those photos Hadley had claimed would prove her affair with Emerson.

However, for them to get the photos—or whatever was in the box—meant taking Laney off the ranch and all the way to Austin. That wasn't his first choice of things to do when someone had already attacked her. She'd be out in the open where hired guns could come at her.

"Talk to the bank manager again," Owen told Kellan. Laney moved closer to him, no doubt so she could listen to the phone conversation Owen was having with his brother. He considered putting the call on speaker, but the truth was, he didn't mind her being this close to him. It eased his suddenly frayed nerves more than it should. "See if there's a way for us to get access to the box without Laney actually being there."

From the other end of the line Owen heard his brother sigh. "I already asked. Or rather, I demanded, and he said Laney had to come in person with a picture ID. Either that, or we have to go the search-warrant route."

Owen had expected that to be the manager's response, but he still cursed. "Try again." He dragged in a long breath. "Emerson just left here, and I don't like the way things are starting to play out. He claims someone's trying to blackmail him."

"Blackmail? Did Emerson admit to the affair with Hadley?" Kellan quickly asked.

"No. He denied it. He's got a recording of the blackmailer's demand. This might not have anything to do with Laney, but I don't like the timing."

"Neither do I," Kellan agreed. "I'll call the bank manager one more time and see what I can do." His brother paused. "How deep do you think Emerson is involved in this?"

Judging from Laney's expression, she wanted to say "very," but Owen still wasn't sure. "Emerson gave us permission to look into his financials," Owen settled for saying. "I'd like to get that started."

"You think Emerson could have paid for those hired guns?" Kellan pressed.

"I just want to be able to rule it out, and this is a start." Maybe not a good start, though, because someone as smart as Emerson could have a hidden account. No way would he have paid for hired killers out of his checking account and then offered to let Owen take a look at it.

"Yeah," Kellan said a moment later, both agreement and concern in his tone. "I'll let you know what the bank manager says."

When Owen ended the call, he turned back to Laney and saw exactly what he figured would be there. Hope with a hefty layering of fear. "I'll have to go to the bank," she insisted before he could say anything. "I need to see what's in that safe-deposit box, and me being there is the fastest way to do this."

She did need to see the contents of the box. So did he, but Owen was still hoping the bank manager would come through and Laney could then view the box through a video feed. *Safely* view it. Owen stared at her, trying to come up with some argument that would convince her of that, but he drew a blank on anything he could say to change her mind.

A blank about the argument anyway.

Unfortunately his mind came up with all sorts of other possibilities. None good. But plenty of them were pretty bad. Because they involved kissing her again. Heck, they involved taking her to bed.

Silently cursing himself, Owen slipped his arm around her waist and pulled her to him. Since Jack was only a few yards away and still at the window, his brother would no doubt see the embrace and give him grief about it later. But this was like the close contact he'd gotten from Laney when she'd been listening to Kellan's call. Owen needed this, too.

Apparently, Laney needed it as well, because she sighed and moved in closer.

Owen didn't dare pull back and look at her since that would have absolutely led to a kiss, but he pressed her against him and let the now-familiar feel of her settle him. Ironic that Laney would be able to do that.

The settling didn't last, though. That was because the other thoughts came. The guilt. The feeling that he was somehow cheating on his wife. Again, ironic. Naomi wouldn't have wanted him to go even this long without seeking out someone else. He'd been the one not willing to jump back into those waters.

Until now.

Owen might have considered that progress if it hadn't been stupid to get involved with someone in his protective custody.

His phone rang, thankfully putting a stop to any other thoughts about kissing Laney. He frowned when he saw the caller. Not Kellan. But rather Terrance. Laney frowned, too, and that expression only deepened when Owen answered.

"Ask Laney what the hell she thinks she's doing," Terrance snarled the moment he was on the line.

"Anything specific, or is this just a general rant?" Owen countered.

"Yes, it's specific. Someone's following me, and I figure she's responsible. The Longview Ridge Sheriff's Office doesn't have probable cause to put a tail on me."

"You're wrong about that. You're on probation, and you're a person of interest in an attack. We have a right to tail you."

But that was just a reminder, not something that'd actually happened. Kellan hadn't put a deputy on Terrance. He glanced at Laney just to make sure she hadn't hired someone to do that, and she shook her head. Not that Owen had thought for one second that she would without talking to him.

"Who's following you?" Owen asked Terrance.

"How the hell should I know? Someone who's driving a dark blue sedan. I figure it's either your man or Laney's. Maybe one of her PI friends."

"Well, it's not. I would say it's your imagination, but since you've got a lot of experience putting tails on people, you should know the real thing when you see it. Where are you?" Owen asked, not waiting for Terrance to gripe about the comment he'd just made.

"My lawyer and I are on the interstate, and the car's been following us for about ten miles now. You're sure it's not someone you know?"

"No," Laney and Owen answered in unison.

He would have pushed Terrance for more info

than just the vague response "on the interstate," but Terrance hung up.

"It could be a ruse," Laney immediately said. "Terrance might think he'll be less of a person of interest if he makes us believe someone's after him."

Owen couldn't agree more, but he had to look at this from both sides. They had two other persons of interest: Emerson and Nettie. If one of them was guilty, then Terrance would make a fine patsy, and they could pin all of this on him.

He was about to put his phone away, but it rang again. This time it was Kellan so he answered immediately. Owen put the call on speaker so that Jack would be able to hear.

"It's a no-go from the bank manager," Kellan told them right away. "He needs Laney there with her ID. If not, then we have to wait for the warrant."

Owen didn't even bother to groan since it was the answer he'd expected. "How close are we to getting the warrant?"

"It could come through later today now that we've got the box narrowed down. Still, the bank manager is saying if the key doesn't match, then he'll fight the warrant. Apparently, Hadley emphasized that condition in writing when she set up the safe-deposit box."

Hadley had likely done that as a precaution, to make sure no one got into it by posing as Laney or her.

"There should be two keys," Kellan noted. "The second one wasn't found on Hadley's body or in her apartment or vehicle. Any idea who she would have given the other key to?"

Since that question was obviously aimed at Laney, Owen just looked at her.

"No," Laney admitted. "She didn't actually give one to me. I found this one when I was going through her things." She paused. "But it's possible she had the key with her when she died, and if so, the killer could have taken it."

Kellan didn't disagree. Neither did Owen.

"But her killer might not have known the location of the bank," Laney added. "He or she might have been looking for it all this time."

Again, that was true, and Owen only hoped the killer had managed to get to it before they did.

"Jack and I will drive Laney to the bank," Owen explained to Kellan. "You're still planning on meeting us there?"

"Yeah. I'll have one of the deputies with me," Kellan assured him, and he ended the call.

Four lawmen. Maybe that would be enough.

Jack went to the front door, opened it and glanced around. He still had his gun drawn. Owen did the same, waiting until Jack gave the nod before he took hold of Laney's arm to hurry her to the cruiser. It wasn't far, only about fifteen feet away, but it still meant being out in the open.

Jack went ahead of them but stayed close, and Owen positioned Laney in between them. The bad feeling in the pit of his stomach hit him hard just as they reached the bottom step. It wasn't enough of a warning, though, for him to do anything about it.

Because the shot blasted through the air.

THE SOUND OF the shot barely had time to register in Laney's mind when Owen hooked his arm around her and dragged her to the ground.

Her pulse jumped, racing like the adrenaline that surged through her. Sweet heaven. Someone was trying to kill them again.

Just ahead of them, Jack dropped, too, and both Owen and he fired glances around, no doubt looking for the shooter. Laney forced herself to do the same, though it was hard for her to see much of anything because Owen had positioned his body over hers.

Another shot came, slamming into the ground between Jack and them. Laney couldn't be sure, but she thought the gunshots had come from her left, where there was a pasture.

And trees.

Some of the oaks were wide enough to conceal a gunman. If so, he was in a bad position. Well, bad for them. Because he would have a clear shot if they tried to get to the cruiser. He'd have just as clear a shot if they tried to scramble back onto the porch. They were trapped and with very little cover.

"There," Jack said, tipping his head toward one of the oaks.

Dear Reader,

Since you are a lover of our books, your opinions are important to us... and so is your time.

That's why we made sure your **"FAST FIVE" READER SURVEY** can be completed in just a few minutes. Your answers to the five questions will help us remain at the forefront of women's fiction.

And, as a thank-you for participating, we'd like to send you **4 FREE THANK-YOU GIFTS!**

Enjoy your gifts with our appreciation,

Pam Powers

Chapter Nine

Owen stood in the observation room of the sheriff's office and watched Laney as she gave Kellan her statement about the attack. Owen had already done his report, but each word he'd written had only fueled his rage. It didn't soothe his temper one bit hearing and seeing Laney replay the ordeal.

He wanted to curse himself, but he didn't even know where to start. He'd screwed up way too many things today—things that could have gotten people killed.

Here, he'd ignored his gut instinct and allowed Laney to be put in yet another dangerous situation. One that had not only involved his brother but also his daughter. All those shots had been fired way too close to the house and Addie.

Owen had known it hadn't been a good idea to take Laney to the bank, had known her being out in the open was just asking for trouble. And trouble was exactly what they'd gotten.

However, that was only the start of things that he'd botched. The driver of the SUV that had nearly killed them had also gotten away. Now the ranch was yet another crime scene, and he had nothing to show for it. No shooter and no safe way to get Laney to Austin. Whoever was after her would just use that trip to make another attempt on her life.

When he saw Laney push back from the table and stand, Owen went back into the hall so he could see her. She wasn't crying, wasn't shaking. That was something at least, and she looked less on edge than he felt.

"Still beating yourself up?" she asked, sliding a hand down his arm.

Kellan came out of the room, his glance at Owen connecting long enough for them to have one of those silent brotherly conversations. At the end of it, Kellan only lifted an eyebrow.

"Laney held up just fine," his brother told him before he headed back to his office.

Owen was glad about the "holding up" part, but it didn't let him off the hook. "I deserve some beating up," he told her.

Laney made eye contact, too, but it was more than a long glance with those baby blues. "You saved my life" was all she said before she leaned in and brushed a kiss on his mouth.

He didn't know what stunned him more, the kiss or the fact that she seemed sincerely grateful even though he'd nearly gotten her and others killed by not listening to that bad feeling he'd had in his gut.

"I can see you don't want my thanks," she whispered. "You want to beat yourself up for something that was out of your control. Should I beat myself up, too? After all, I'm the reason for the danger."

Owen cursed. "I knew it was a mistake to try to take you to the bank."

"I pushed you into it," Laney insisted and then paused. "Maybe we can beat ourselves up together?"

Laney added what might have been a smile to that, but he didn't want any attempt at being light-hearted right now. He was angry...and scared. Because no matter what he did, he might not be able to keep Addie, Laney and the others safe.

She stayed close, right against him, while she looked up at him. She seemed to be holding her breath as if waiting for something.

Behind them, he could hear the chatter in the squad room. Could also hear Kellan talking to someone on the phone. There was so much to do with this new investigation, but he didn't budge. Owen just stood there. Until he gave up on the notion of common sense.

And he kissed her.

He instantly felt the relief, the tension, draining from his body. Of course, he got a tension of a different kind. The heat from the attraction. But he didn't care. Right now, he just needed this, and he was pretty sure Laney needed it, too.

She moved against him, slipping right into his arms. Moving into the kiss, too. He took in her taste, her scent, and likely would've have taken a lot more than he should have if he hadn't heard the footsteps.

Owen pulled away from her and turned to see Gunnar coming toward them. If his fellow deputy had seen the kiss, then he wisely didn't say anything about it.

"I just had another go at questioning Gilley," Gunnar explained.

Owen certainly hadn't forgotten about the hired gun they had in a holding cell, but he'd moved the man to the back burner. He was glad, though, that Gunnar hadn't because right now Gilley was the one person who might be able to give them answers.

"Please tell me that Gilley's talking," Owen said.

Gunnar shook his head, but then he shrugged. "He's not talking about the attack, but when I mentioned that someone had tried to kill Laney and you again, he didn't exactly seem pleased about that. He got nervous and then demanded to speak to Emerson."

"Emerson?" Laney and Owen repeated at the same time.

"Did Gilley say why he wanted to see him?" Owen asked.

"No, but I figure Gilley's still wanting a plea deal, and he wants to go straight to the source."

Maybe. But with everything that had gone on, Owen had to wonder if Gilley wanted to talk to his boss, the man who'd hired him. And that man could be Emerson.

"I called Emerson to let him know about the *request*," Gunnar went on, "but he didn't answer, so I left him a voice mail." Gunnar stared at him. "You don't think it's a good idea for Emerson to see Gilley?"

Kellan had almost certainly filled Gunnar in on the investigation. All aspects of it. But it was possible that Gunnar didn't know that Owen now considered the DA a suspect in Hadley's murder.

"No, it could be a very good idea." Owen thought about it for a second. "But if Emerson shows for that talk, I'd like to be here to listen."

Gunnar nodded, started to walk away and then turned back. "Jack checked out the car that Terrance said was following him, but when he didn't get any hits, he went ahead to the ranch. He said he figured you'd want him to be there with Addie and the others."

Good. He did indeed want his brother at the ranch to make sure Addie stayed safe. Maybe the same at-large gunman was the one who'd attacked them, but it was just as possible there were several of the hired thugs. Either that or the shooter had manager to get away from the tree and into that SUV darn fast.

"I need to get some paperwork done," Owen told Laney after Gunnar had left. "You should try to get some rest in the break room."

She shook her head. "I can work, too, if I can borrow a computer. I need to touch base with the San Antonio cops to see if they're making progress on Joe's murder. I also want to contact some people who knew him and try to come up with a lead." She paused, met his gaze. "It's very likely that his killer and our attackers are one and the same."

Owen couldn't dispute that. He hated that her mind would be on murder when she was clearly exhausted, but if their positions had been reversed, he'd be doing the same thing. Any thread they could latch onto right now could lead them to an arrest and put an end to the danger.

"You can use my desk," he offered as they headed for the squad room. "I'll work in Kellan's office with him. Just stay away from the windows."

And Owen hated that he had to add a reminder like that. Not while the memories of the most recent nightmare were so fresh. Still, they had to take precautions even in the sheriff's office since one of their suspects was the district attorney who could easily gain access to the building.

"You do the same." Laney stopped as if she might say something else. Or kiss him again. But then she managed a thin smile before she went to his desk.

Kellan was on the phone when Owen walked into

his office. Owen didn't know who he was talking to but, judging from his brother's tight jaw, it wasn't a pleasant conversation. Kellan wrote something down on a notepad, finished the call and stared at the phone for a few seconds before he put it away and looked at Owen.

"The link for the eavesdropping device was on one of the computers we took from Nettie and Emerson's house," Kellan finally said. "Specifically, it was on Nettie's laptop."

Owen understood his brother's tight jaw. Oh, man. This wasn't going to be pretty.

"The techs got not only a date but the exact time of installation." Kellan passed him the notepad and Owen saw that the software had been put on the computer less than a week earlier at four thirty in the afternoon. "Obviously, I'll need to get both Emerson and Nettie in here to see if they have alibis."

"They do," Owen immediately said. "That's when they had a big birthday barbecue for Nettie. I even dropped by with Addie." Owen cursed. "And that means Emerson and Nettie will claim one of the guests or someone from the catering company could have slipped inside and done this."

"Yeah," Kellan grumbled profanely. "I don't have to ask if you saw anyone suspicious."

Owen dragged a hand through his hair and tried to pull up the memories of the party. "No, but there were a lot of people that I didn't know. Some of

Nettie's old college friends and some of Emerson's business associates. Addie was fussy—teething," he added, "so I didn't stay long. Only about half an hour."

Still, Owen would go back through what he could remember of the day to see if there was anything to recall. One thing was for sure, he hadn't remembered anyone who'd looked like a hired thug. That would have certainly snagged his attention.

Kellan put his hands on his hips. "Let's go with the theory that Nettie knew about her husband's affair. An affair that her husband claims never happened. But maybe she wants to know for sure, and the best way for her to do that is to listen in on what Laney is saying."

"And have a look at her computer files," Owen piped in, agreeing with his brother's theory.

Kellan nodded. "Nettie could have hired someone to put the program on her computer, and the party would have been a good cover. Her hired man could just pose as part of the catering crew or a guest. Or Nettie could have even slipped away and installed the software herself."

Both were possible. Ditto for Emerson being able to do it, as well. No one would have thought anything about the host disappearing for the handful of minutes it would have taken to plant the device.

So they were right back to square one. Not a good

place to be with the possibility of another attack looming over them.

"The next question is how Joe Henshaw fits into this," Owen noted, still going with Kellan's train of thought.

Maybe Laney had heard him say her assistant's name because she hurried to the doorway and volleyed glances at both of them. "What happened?"

Owen and Kellan looked at each other and Kellan gave him the go-ahead nod to answer her question.

"The eavesdropping software was on Nettie's computer," Owen explained. Then he filled her in on the time of the installation and the party that either Nettie or Emerson could have used as an alibi.

When he finished, Laney's only reaction was a long exhale of breath. Obviously the news wasn't a surprise to her, so the frustration he was seeing on her face was for him. Because she knew it wasn't easy for a member of his family to be a murder suspect.

"I don't know if Joe found something to link Nettie or Emerson to Hadley's murder," she said after she'd taken a moment to absorb everything. "I've been going through his files, and I haven't found anything like that. Maybe Nettie or Emerson didn't want to risk him, or me, learning something."

Owen tried to wrap his mind around Nettie and Emerson committing cold-blooded murder. He couldn't, but they likely hadn't been the ones to put the bullets in Joe. Maybe hadn't even been the ones who'd personally murdered Hadley. However, they could have hired someone to do their dirty work.

"Emerson gave us permission to review his financials," Owen reminded Kellan.

Kellan nodded again. "I got them just a couple of minutes ago. Nothing pops, but I haven't had time to take a close look."

"I can do that for you," Owen offered. But Emerson's bank accounts were only half of the picture. "Is the eavesdropping software enough for us to get into Nettie's accounts?"

The sound Kellan made let Owen know even with that kind of connection, it wasn't going to be easy, but he took out his phone anyway. It rang before Kellan could make a call.

"It's Austin PD," Kellan relayed to them. He didn't put it on speaker, but whatever the caller said to him had Kellan blowing out what sounded to be a breath of relief. Relief that didn't last long, though. "No. That's not a good idea. There's been another attack, and it's not safe." He paused, obviously listening, and ended the call with "Good. I'll get right on that."

"What happened?" Owen immediately asked.

Kellan typed something on his laptop keyboard. "The search warrant on the bank came through, *finally*, and since it's not safe for Laney to go there, I convinced the Austin cops to do a video feed for us when they open the box."

Owen didn't exactly cheer, but that was what he felt like doing. He'd wanted to know what was in that box without putting Laney in harm's way, and this was the best way to do it.

"I'm setting up the feed now," Kellan explained. He continued to work on the laptop while he turned the screen so that all three of them could see it.

Laney automatically moved in closer and, while she didn't say anything, Owen knew this had to feel like a victory for her. She'd been looking for this safe-deposit box for months because she believed it held the photos that would confirm her theory that Emerson had killed Hadley.

And maybe it would.

Owen certainly wasn't feeling victorious about that. Yes, if Emerson had indeed murdered Laney's sister, he wanted the man brought to justice. But that wasn't going to be easy when the photos might only prove an affair and nothing else. Of course, it was possible Hadley had something else in there.

As they waited, Laney took hold of his hand just as the images and sounds popped up on the computer screen. The audio feed crackled with static, but Owen had no trouble seeing the two uniformed cops go into the vault area. Owen didn't know who was operating the camera, but it didn't pan around much. The focus stayed on the box that a guy in a suit—probably the bank manager—pulled from one of the slots in the wall.

The suit set the box on a plain table that reminded Owen of the ones they used in the interview rooms, and he took out a key.

"Is that the key we got from Laney Martin?" Kellan asked the cop.

The uniform nodded and, several moments later, they had confirmation that it was when the manager used it to open it the box.

The person holding the camera immediately moved closer, zooming in on the interior.

Owen immediately cursed when he saw what was inside.

Chapter Ten

Empty.

That definitely hadn't been what Laney had expected when the bank manager opened the box. Nothing. Not even a scrap of paper.

Her thoughts immediately started to run wild.

"Maybe it's not the right box." Laney threw the possibility out there.

Owen made a sound of agreement. Kellan wasn't paying attention because he was already on the phone with the bank manager.

The cops cut the video feed, leaving her to stare at the blank screen. Mercy. Why couldn't there just have been pictures inside? Or something that would have confirmed what Hadley had told her about the affair with Emerson? Now they had nothing, no reason to go after Emerson so they could stop another attack.

If Emerson was to blame, that was.

"My name was on the box," she added, talking

more to herself than Owen. Still, he answered her, along with sliding a soothing hand down her back.

"It was the right key," he pointed out, "but Hadley could have moved the contents."

That was possible, but it didn't answer why her sister would have done that, especially without telling Laney. After all, Hadley had volunteered the info about the pictures, but maybe she'd been murdered before she could let Laney know they'd been moved.

Kellan was cursing when he finished his call. "The bank manager said someone—a woman—accessed the box yesterday."

That got her attention and Laney's gaze shifted from the laptop to him. *Yesterday.* So, Hadley hadn't been the one to empty the box. But that left them with a huge question of who exactly had done that.

"Any reason the bank manager didn't tell us this sooner?" Laney demanded.

"He claims that he couldn't release any info about it until he had the search warrant." Kellan glanced down at the notes he'd taken during the call. "The person had a picture ID with Hadley's name, and she must have also had a key."

"The missing second key," Laney said under her breath. She wanted to blurt out some of that same profanity Kellan was using. "And she must have used a fake ID or one that she stole from Hadley when the key was taken."

Kellan stared at her. "Could Hadley have given the second key to someone else?"

Her mind was whirling so it was hard to think, but Laney forced herself to focus. "She could have perhaps given it to Joe." But almost immediately she had to wave that off. "He would have told me if she'd done that—especially after she was murdered. He would have known it could be critical to finding her killer."

So, not Joe, but maybe a friend. Still, a friend should have come forward by now, which led Laney to consider that Hadley's killer might have taken the key. The only problem with that was why the killer had waited all this time to access the box.

"Hadley might have left it at Joe's place without him knowing," Owen suggested several moments later. Obviously they were all trying to work this out.

That was possible, but another thought flashed into her mind. Not a good thought, either. "Joe had... feelings for Hadley. Actually, I think he was in love with her. So, if she gave him the key and asked him to keep it a secret, he might have, especially since he knew I had found a key in her apartment."

Still, she was going with the theory that Joe hadn't known. And that the person who'd murdered him had searched his place, maybe found the key and then used it. That would explain why the killer had taken so long to get into the box. Maybe a female killer. Maybe Nettie.

Of course, it was just as likely that Terrance or Emerson had hired a woman to pose as Hadley.

"The timing works," Owen said as if reading her thoughts. "Whoever broke into Joe's could have gotten the key and used it to go to the bank."

She shook her head. "But how would the person have known which bank?" Laney stopped, her eyes widening. "Terrance. He had the PI report, so he knew the location."

Owen was taking out his phone to call Terrance before she'd even finished. Because she was right next to him, she heard the unanswered rings and, a few seconds later, the voice mail message. Owen left a message for Terrance to call him back ASAP. Whether the man would actually do that was anyone's guess. If he was guilty, Terrance might even go on the run rather than answer any questions that could lead to his arrest.

"I'll get the footage on the security cameras from the bank, and that way we can see who went in there. I also want Terrance's financials," Kellan grumbled. "And on any other PI reports he might not have shared with us." He looked at Laney. "Do you still have any PI contacts?"

"I do. You want me to make some calls to see if Terrance hired anyone else that he hasn't told us about?"

Kellan nodded. "I'm especially interested if he had a female investigator who could have passed for your sister. Of course, he wouldn't need a PI for that because he could have hired anyone, but we might get lucky."

It was a long shot, but at this point, it was all they had. Laney went back to Owen's desk where she'd left the loaner laptop and got to work, finding contact numbers for every PI she could think of. Too bad her cell phone had been taken in the break-in because she'd had plenty of the numbers in it.

Laney had just finished a list when the front door flew open. Owen came rushing out of Kellan's office and he automatically stepped in front of her and drew his weapon. But it wasn't a hired gun who'd come there to attack them.

It was Emerson.

Along with being out of breath, the DA looked disheveled. His suit was wrinkled, his hair messed up, and there was a fine layer of sweat on his forehead. He opened his mouth and then glanced around at the two other deputies and the dispatcher before he motioned toward Kellan's office.

"We need to talk," Emerson said, his voice a little shaky.

Owen studied him for a couple of seconds before he got moving, staying between Emerson and Laney as they entered Kellan's office. Emerson immediately shut the door.

"The blackmailer called me again." Emerson took

out his phone, put it on Kellan's desk in front of him and hit the play button.

"Time's run out, DA," the caller said. It was the same mechanical voice they'd heard before. "You've got an hour to get me that fifty thousand or I tell your sweet wife what's going on. No routing number this time. I want cash, and I'll be in touch as to where you can leave the money."

Kellan listened to it again and checked the time on the call. "It's already been nearly an hour."

Emerson nodded. "I figure he'll call me back any minute now. I don't have the money," he quickly added.

"You shouldn't be paying him anyway," Owen insisted. He moved so that Emerson and he were eye to eye. "You need to tell Nettie. That won't give this snake anything to hold over you. It'd be a lot better for her to hear it from you than him."

Obviously that wasn't the solution Emerson wanted because he huffed. Then he groaned and squeezed his eyes shut for a moment. "Nettie could believe the lie about the affair. She could leave me because of it."

"Maybe," Owen said. "But she's going to find out one way or another." He paused. "Besides, Nettie might have her own secrets."

"What do you mean?" Emerson snapped, his attention slicing to Owen.

Owen dragged in a long breath. "Go home, Emerson, and talk to your wife."

Emerson's stare turned into a glare. He held it for so long that Owen figured the man was about to have a burst of temper. But Emerson finally just shook his head. "I want to clear up this mess with the blackmailer first." His gaze shifted to Kellan and now there was some temper in his eyes. "If you can't or won't help me, then I'll have to handle it myself."

"I wouldn't advise that," Kellan told him.

Emerson's glare intensified as he snatched up his phone, obviously ready to storm out.

But Owen stopped him. "Rohan Gilley wants to talk to you."

Laney studied Emerson's expression, and she figured Owen and Kellan were doing the same. Something went through his eyes, something she couldn't quite peg. Frustration maybe? Or maybe something more. Fear? Of course, she could just be projecting that.

"I don't have time for Gilley right now," Emerson snapped. "Tell him that. Tell him I'll get back here when I have some things settled."

Emerson walked out, leaving Laney to wonder if that had been some kind of assurance or even a veiled threat for the gunman.

Kellan sighed. "I need to get both Nettie and him in here, *together*, for a face-to-face interview. An official one where I ask some hard questions. I think a good air clearing might help all the way around since both of them have motives for the attacks."

Owen shook his head when Gunnar stepped in the office doorway. "Emerson won't be talking to Gilley for a while," he told his fellow deputy.

"I'll let him know, but that's not why I'm here." Gunnar paused. "It's bad news. We have a dead body."

OWEN STARED AT the photo the Austin PD had just sent them and felt the punch of dread when he saw the dead woman's face. A face he'd seen on the surveillance footage that the bank had sent over earlier. He had no doubts that she'd been the same person who'd gotten into the safe-deposit box with Hadley's fake ID.

And now she wouldn't be able to tell them what she'd taken or where it was.

Laney touched her fingers to her mouth as she studied the photo, and Owen saw her blink hard. No doubt fighting tears. "She doesn't look like my sister. Not really."

No. The hair color was the same, but that was about all. It was something the woman could have easily dyed to come closer to a physical match for the person she'd been impersonating.

"What happened to her?" Laney asked, glancing at Gunnar before her gaze went back to the photo.

"Two gunshot wounds to the chest," Gunnar explained. "Point-blank range. She had two IDs on her. One in your sister's name and the other was her own driver's license. Her prints were in the system, so they were able to confirm her identity as Nancy Flanery."

Laney's forehead creased, and she repeated the name as if trying to recall where she'd heard it before. "It sounds familiar, but I don't recognize her."

"Austin PD's running a background check now. I'm doing the same," Gunnar added a moment later. "She's from San Antonio and is a criminal informant."

That got Owen's attention. "A CI?" he said under his breath. "For Austin PD?"

"San Antonio," Gunnar clarified. "She has a record for drug possession, but her latest arrest was three years ago. She seems to have stayed clean since then. Or maybe she just hadn't gotten caught."

Either was possible. Obviously she had crossed paths with someone who'd either paid her to impersonate Hadley or had forced or coerced her into doing it.

"Someone must have hired her to go to that bank," Laney said.

That was Owen's top theory, too. Hired her, used her to get their hands on the photos and then murdered her so that she wouldn't be able to tell the cops who'd paid her to get into that safe-deposit box.

"Oh, and I thought this was interesting..." Gunnar continued, reading from his notes. "According to the preliminary report, Nancy Flanery had gunshot residue on her hands, but there was no weapon found on her."

Owen thought about that for a second. "Maybe because her killer took it. But she could have gotten off a shot first."

With luck, perhaps she could have even wounded her attacker. If so, Austin PD might find blood other than the victim's at the crime scene.

Laney went into the squad room and brought back the laptop she'd been working on. "Let me do a search of my files to see if anything pops up. Like I said, her name sounds familiar, so it's possible she was connected to one of my investigations."

She put the laptop on Kellan's desk and, leaning over, typed in "Nancy Flanery." She frowned when nothing came up. "Let me switch to Joe's files." Laney repeated the process.

Then she froze.

"She's here." Laney turned the screen so that Kellan, Gunnar and Owen would better be able to see it. "A week ago Joe talked to her after he'd gotten a tip that she knew something about Hadley's killer. Nancy claimed she didn't, but Joe apparently didn't believe her." She tapped the screen to show the triple question marks Joe had added at the end of the short report.

"Did you ever meet this woman?" Kellan asked.

"No. I'm almost positive I didn't. According to these notes, this was the first time Joe had met with her. Since it was only a week ago, I was already at Owen's. I didn't do any interviews after I moved there."

She looked at Owen and once again he saw the apology in her eyes. He definitely didn't like that she'd lied to him, but with the attacks, he knew why she had been so cautious.

"Do you think she's the one who killed Joe?" Laney asked. "If she's working for the person who attacked us, then she could have gone after Joe." But she waved that off. "I know it's a long shot."

It was, but it could still be a connection. Joe might not have had his guard up if someone he'd known had approached him, and it was possible Nancy had murdered Joe and then gone to the bank in Austin. The timing would work. If she had indeed committed murder and then fraud, the woman would have been a bad loose end.

And it had likely gotten her killed.

"I'll try to put a rush on that background check," Gunnar offered. He headed back into the squad room just as Kellan's phone rang.

Kellan scrubbed his hand over his face and showed them the name on the screen. Nettie. After blowing out a huff of frustration, he answered the call and put it on speaker.

"Emerson's missing," Nettie blurted out before

Kellan could even issue a greeting. Her voice was practically a shout. "You've got to find him now."

"Nettie, he's not missing," Kellan assured her. "He was just here in my office."

She made a hoarse sob. "He's there? I need to talk to him."

"He left already." Kellan huffed again. "I was hoping he'd go home to you."

"He hasn't been here. What did he say?" Nettie demanded, her words running together.

Owen could tell from his brother's expression that Kellan was trying to figure out how to answer that. He took several moments and the woman continued to cry. "What's this about, Nettie?"

Nettie took a couple of moments, as well. "His assistant said Emerson was very upset, that he grabbed some things from his desk and practically ran out. She'd never seen him like that, and was worried about him, so she let me know about it. But when I tried to call him, he didn't answer. Something's wrong, and you need to find him now."

That didn't help ease the frustration on Kellan's face. "I'll see what I can do. If I find out anything, I'll let you know."

"Emerson could be meeting with the blackmailer," Laney said the moment Kellan ended the call with Nettie.

Kellan made a sound of agreement and stepped out into the squad room. "Raylene," he said, speaking to one of the deputies, Raylene McNeal. "I need you to find Emerson. Make some calls, ask around, see what you can come up with."

Since Raylene had witnessed Emerson storming out earlier, she didn't seem especially surprised by the request. She just nodded and took out her phone.

Owen was about to volunteer to help, but he saw their visitor walking toward the front door. Terrance. The moment he was inside, he flicked Laney a glance before his attention zoomed to Owen.

"I couldn't take your call, but your voice mail sounded...urgent," Terrance said. "What can I do to help?" As usual, there was a chilly layer of indifference in his tone and expression.

"It is urgent," Owen assured him. "A woman was murdered, and I want to know if one of your PI tails happened to see her."

Terrance shrugged his shoulders. "I can ask them, but why would they have done that? Does this dead woman have a connection to Laney?"

Owen held off on answering. Instead he turned the computer screen toward Terrance so he could see the photo Austin PD had sent them. "Her name is Nancy Flanery."

The indifference vanished and Terrance whirled toward Laney. This time, there was fiery anger in his eyes. "What kind of sick game are you playing?" he demanded.

That rage was in his voice, too. So much rage

that Owen actually stepped between Laney and him. Laney didn't let that last long, though. She moved to Owen's side and faced Terrance head-on.

"I'm not playing a game," Laney insisted. "Do you know that woman?"

Terrance had to get his jaw unclenched before he spoke. "Are you trying to set me up?"

Owen figured Laney looked as surprised as he did. "Why would you think that?" Owen demanded.

Terrance jabbed his index finger at the picture on the screen. "Because Nancy works for me."

Chapter Eleven

Laney wasn't sure what she'd expected Terrance to say, but that wasn't it. She shook her head. "Nancy was a criminal informant."

Terrance groaned and, with his gaze back on Nancy's picture, sank into the chair next to Kellan's desk. Laney couldn't tell if he was genuinely upset or if this was all some kind of act.

"Nancy sold info to the cops every now and then," Terrance admitted. "But I'd also hired her to keep an ear out for any information about Hadley's murder." He looked at Laney again and some of his anger rekindled. "I figured eventually you'd try to pin your sister's death on me. Just to get back at me. If you ended up doing that, I wanted some ammunition I could use to defend myself."

Laney didn't take her gaze from his. "I want to find her actual killer, not simply *pin* it on someone."

"Right," he said as if he didn't believe her. He

tipped his head to the photo. "Who did that to her? Who killed her?"

Owen stepped closer, standing directly in front of Terrance. "That's what we're trying to find out. Start talking. When's the last time you saw her?"

It was a simple enough question, but it only seemed to bring Terrance's rage. "I didn't kill her, and I refuse to stay here and be accused of it." He sprang to his feet, obviously ready to bolt, but Owen took hold of his arm to stop him.

"You can either answer that here, or I'll arrest you for obstruction of justice and withholding evidence," Owen warned him. "Then you'll wait in a holding cell until Austin PD can come and pick you up."

Terrance slung off his grip with far more force than was necessary before he got right in Owen's face. "Are you doing Laney's bidding now? Her witch hunt?" Terrance practically spit the words out.

"I'm asking a question." Owen definitely didn't back down. "One that it sounds like you're evading. When's the last time you saw Nancy?"

They continued to glare at each other for several long seconds before Terrance ground out some raw profanity and dropped back a step. "Three days ago. She called to say she needed some cash and wondered if I had any jobs for her. I told her I didn't, but that if I found something, I'd get back to her." He paused. "Did she do something stupid to get the money she needed?"

"It looks that way," Owen conceded. "Posing as Hadley, she went into the very bank where your PI had followed Hadley shortly before she was killed."

Terrance cursed again, but this time when he spoke, his voice was much softer. "Someone obviously hired Nancy to do that and then killed her after she'd finished the job. And no, it wasn't me," he quickly added. He shook his head. "I wouldn't have had a PI on her or the bank so I can't tell you who did this."

Laney considered not just what he'd said but also his body language. Terrance looked and sounded sincere, but this could definitely be an act. If so, then why had he used one of his own employees to get into the bank? Maybe it was some sort of reverse psychology. By putting himself in the center of this, he perhaps thought it would make him appear innocent.

Laney had no intentions, though, of taking him off her suspect list.

"I'll speak with my PIs," Terrance said, glancing over at Kellan before staring at Owen. "Do you plan to arrest me?"

Owen took his time answering. "Not yet, but we'll need an official statement."

"I'll take it," Kellan volunteered.

Terrance's mouth tightened again. "I'll want my lawyer here."

"Then call him and tell him to get over here

ASAP. Until he arrives, you can stay in the interview room." Kellan led him in that direction.

Laney waited until they were out of earshot before she turned to Owen. "I just don't know if what he said was true," he commented before she could ask. "But even if it was, I still don't trust him."

So they were on the same page and, while it was comforting to have him on her side, they were in a very frustrating position. Someone else was dead and they still didn't have the photos or whatever else her sister had left in the safe-deposit box. Worse, they couldn't arrest anyone to make sure no one else got killed. Or that there were no more attacks on Laney and him.

Owen stared at her a moment, slipped his arm around her and eased her to him. "I'd like to be able to get you out of here, to take you back to my grandparents' house."

She filled in the blanks. Yes, he wanted to do that, but it wasn't safe. "We can stay here as long as necessary." Laney paused. "Maybe we should put out the word that we're here. It could put off someone sending hired guns to the ranch."

He pulled back, met her gaze. "And make ourselves targets. Especially you." Owen cursed softly. "You're thinking of Addie. Thank you for that."

"You don't have to thank me. Of course, I'm thinking about her. I'd rather thugs come after me here than there. In fact, maybe it's time to use me as bait."

This time his profanity wasn't so soft and he jerked away. "No," he snapped. "No." When he repeated it, his voice was a little softer, but filled with just as much emotion. "And that doesn't have a damn thing to do with that kiss. Or this one."

She didn't even see it coming, but his mouth was suddenly on hers. Taking. And his right hand went to the back of her neck, holding her in place. There was no gentleness here, only the raw emotion of the moment. It was rough, punishing, but even then she could feel the heat in it. Could feel the need that it stirred in her.

"No," he repeated for a third time. His hand was still on her neck, his fingers thrust into her hair, and he stayed that way for several moments before he finally backed away from her.

"I just want Addie safe," she managed to say when she gathered enough breath to speak. "I want *you* safe."

The corner of his mouth lifted, but the amusement vanished as quickly as it had come. "Now, that's the kiss talking."

No, it wasn't. It was what she felt for him, but rather than say that, Laney kept things light. "Well, it was a good kiss. Memorable," she added, trying out one of those partial smiles. Like his, hers was short-lived. Because it hadn't been just memorable.

The kiss had been unforgettable.

Owen was unforgettable.

And when this was over and they'd caught the person trying to kill them, she was going to have to deal with not only the aftermath of the violence but also something else. Having her heart broken into a million little pieces.

The thought of having sex with him flashed into her head, and she nearly blurted out that they should go for it at least once so they could burn off some of this fire that was flowing through them. Thankfully, she didn't get the chance to spill all—something she would have no doubt regretted—because someone came in through the front door of the squad room.

Nettie.

Great. Laney didn't have the mental energy to deal with the woman, and she figured Owen didn't, either. But Nettie stopped the moment her attention landed on them. Laney was no longer in Owen's arms, but she realized that he hadn't taken his hand from her hair. He eased his grip away as he turned toward Nettie.

"I'm glad you have time for that sort of thing," Nettie said, irony and bitterness in her voice.

Laney was a little surprised when Owen didn't move away from her. He stayed shoulder to shoulder with her, still touching her as they faced the woman.

"You're supposed to be looking for Emerson," Nettie added. She marched toward them. "But I find you here with your hands on the very person who's responsible for the mess we're in."

"Excuse me?" Laney said at the same moment Owen snarled, "What the hell does that mean?"

"We didn't have trouble until she came here. She lied to you, turned you against Emerson and me, and now Emerson is missing." Each of Nettie's words snapped like a bullwhip, but the fit of temper must have drained her because on a hoarse sob, she sagged against the door frame. "I need to find my husband. Please." She looked at Laney when she added the *please*.

Laney wasn't immune to the woman's pain. That seemed like the real deal. But she didn't trust Nettie any more than she did Terrance or Emerson.

"I take it that Emerson didn't return your call?" Owen asked as he helped Nettie to a chair. He also turned the computer where the photo of the dead woman was still on the screen.

"No. I called him six times. Maybe more. And he hasn't answered." A fresh round of tears came, but Nettie quickly brushed them away. She looked up at him. "Tell me what happened to him. I have to know what's going on." Nettie added another whispered *please*.

Owen stared at her a moment then dragged in a long breath. "Just know that Emerson isn't going to thank me for telling you this." He paused several long moments. "Someone's been trying to blackmail Emerson."

Nettie looked up at him, blinked. Judging from her stunned reaction, she hadn't been expecting that. "Wh-what?"

"A blackmailer who's called him several times to try to extort money from him."

Nettie shook her head and volleyed wide-eyed glances at Laney and him as if looking for any signs this was a joke. "Blackmail him for what?"

Owen just stared at her.

The woman did another round of glancing before she shook her head. "No. My husband didn't have an affair with her sister." She flung an accusing finger at Laney.

Laney figured she was the one who looked surprised now. "What do you know about my sister?" she prompted. Of course, Terrance had said there'd been a meeting between Hadley and Nettie, but Laney hadn't known if he was telling the truth or not.

"I know my husband didn't have an affair with her." Nettie seemed adamant about that, too, and when she got to her feet, she seemed a lot stronger than she had just seconds earlier. "Yes, I've heard talk, but I know it's not true. Emerson wouldn't cheat on me."

Laney didn't argue with her, but she would mention something else. "Why else would someone try to blackmail your husband?"

Nettie's chin came up. "There are plenty of reasons. Emerson's an important man, and he's prosecuted a lot of bad people. One of them could be trying to get some revenge."

"This doesn't seem to be about revenge," Owen quickly pointed out. "Blackmailers usually want money to keep a secret. Of course, they usually end up wanting more and more money."

Nettie stared at him again and Laney thought she was maybe trying to find a reasonable comeback. But Nettie only huffed, "I don't know why someone would demand money. But it's not because he cheated." She started to pace across Kellan's office. "It probably has something to do with that mix-up about the eavesdropping program being on my computer."

It wasn't a mix-up. The program had been there, but obviously Nettie wasn't going to accept responsibility for that.

"Was Emerson upset about that?" Owen asked, sounding very much like a cop who was fishing for information from a potential suspect.

"Of course, he was. But he knows I was set up, that there's no way I would do something like that." Nettie stopped the pacing so she could glare at Laney. "Why would I care about eavesdropping on you anyway?"

Laney didn't even have to think about the answer to that. "Because you're worried that your husband did indeed have an affair with my sister and you wanted to know if I'd found any proof of it."

"No!" Nettie's glare got worse. "I didn't do that because there's no proof to find. I know you want to find your sister's killer, but you'd better keep my husband and me out of your lies."

Owen took Nettie by the shoulders. "What if she's not lying?" he asked. "What if Laney's telling the truth?"

Laney steeled herself for another lash from Nettie's temper, but the woman stilled and shook her head. There was nothing adamant about that head shake, though, and the tears shimmered in Nettie's eyes again.

Owen turned at the sound of footsteps. When Kellan stepped into the doorway, he looked at the three of them, obviously piecing together what had been going on. He motioned for Owen to join him in the squad room and extended the gesture to Laney. They stepped out, but Kellan didn't say anything until he was back in the hall and out of Nettie's earshot.

"Terrance called his PIs," Kellan told them. "All of them claim they hadn't seen Nancy in days and that they don't know who hired her to go into the safe-deposit box."

"You believe them?" Owen asked.

Kellan lifted his shoulder. "Terrance put the calls on speaker so I could hear, and the PIs seemed to be telling the truth. Of course, Terrance could have coached them to say that. After all, we would have found the connection between Nancy and him, and he would have known that would eventually lead to us talking to his PIs."

Yes, it would have, and coaching was something Terrance would have done. He would cover any and all bases rather than go back to jail.

Laney glanced in the direction of his office just to make sure Nettie hadn't come out. She hadn't. "As far as we know, Terrance is the only one of our suspects who knew Nancy."

Kellan nodded. "So, I ask myself, why would he use her? But maybe he did that because he might not be the only one of our suspects with links to Nancy. I want to take a look at Nancy's phone logs and financials that Austin PD will be getting. There might be something there to help us with our investigation."

Laney agreed, and her gaze drifted back to Nettie. "And her financials?"

"I'm working on it," Kellan said with a sigh. He opened his mouth to say more but a loud shout stopped him. It had come from the squad room, and it had both Owen and Kellan drawing their weapons.

"Get out here now!" someone yelled.

Emerson.

Kellan and Owen both moved in front of Laney and rushed into the squad room. From over their shoulders, she immediately saw Emerson. And he wasn't alone. He had a man with him.

Emerson was also armed.

He had a gun pointed at a man he was dragging in by his collar. When Emerson slung the man onto the floor, Laney could see that his hands were tied behind his back.

"I had him meet me," Emerson huffed, his breath gusting. His clothes were torn, too, and there was a bruise forming on his right cheek. "And then I bashed him on the head so I could bring him here."

"Who is he?" Kellan asked.

"The blackmailer." Emerson spit the word out like a profanity. "Arrest him now."

OWEN HAD ALREADY had too many surprises today, but obviously they weren't finished when it came to that.

"Give me the gun," Owen ordered Emerson.

Owen intended to get to the bottom of…well, whatever the heck this was, but he didn't want to start until he got that weapon out of Emerson's hand. That wild look in his brother-in-law's eyes let Owen know this was still a very volatile situation.

"Arrest him now," Emerson repeated.

"I'll start doing that when you give me your weapon," Owen countered. He made a quick check to see if Kellan was still in front of Laney. He was. Kellan also had his arm hooked around Nettie, no doubt to prevent the woman from rushing to her husband.

The fire in Emerson's eyes heated up even more,

and it didn't look as if he had any intentions of surrendering the weapon. Not until Nettie spoke.

"Emerson, you're hurt," she said, her voice cracking. "He needs an ambulance," she snarled to Kellan.

Emerson glanced at his wife, at the man on the
floor, and seemed to realize what he'd just done. He
passed the gun to Owen, and Owen handed it off to
Gunnar.

"What happened?" Owen asked Emerson.

But he didn't get a chance to answer. Nettie broke
away from Kellan and ran to her husband. She landed
right in his arms. Owen considered pulling them
apart so he could pat down Emerson for other weapons, but Kellan came forward to do that. Judging
from both his and Nettie's glares, neither cared much
for that.

"He needs an ambulance," Nettie repeated. She
was crying now, but they all ignored her. Even Emerson. Though she did gently touch her fingers to
that bruise on his face.

"I did what I needed to do," Emerson snapped.
"What you wouldn't do." He glanced at both Owen
and Kellan when he added that. "He was blackmailing me, and I put a stop to it."

"I wasn't blackmailing him," the man insisted.
There was a bruise on his cheek as well, and the
anger radiated over every inch of his face. "I told
this nutjob he has it all wrong."

"He met me to take the money that he'd demanded," Emerson insisted. "I didn't have the cash, but I'd stuffed some newspapers in a big envelope to make him think I had it. That's how I got him close enough to hit him."

"I didn't know it was blackmail," the man snapped. "I was just doing somebody a favor."

A bagman. Or else he was claiming to be one.

"Who are you?" Owen demanded. He hauled the man to his feet so he could pat him down. No weapons, and his hands had been secured with a pair of plastic cuffs.

"Norman Perry." The sour tone matched his expression.

"Running him now," Gunnar volunteered.

While Owen waited for Gunnar to do that, Nettie looked up at her husband. "What happened? Why would this man be trying to blackmail you?"

It wasn't a question Owen had intended to ask—because he already knew the answer—so he paused to give Emerson a chance to tell his wife. Emerson certainly didn't jump to do that. He took his time while he looked at everyone in the room but Nettie.

"Someone lied and said I did something I didn't do," Emerson finally said. He tipped his head to Perry. "He had a gun, but I took it from him. It's in my car, and it's unlocked out front."

"I'll get it." Gunnar volunteered. He had his phone pressed to his ear as he went out.

With a firm hold on Perry's arm, Owen led him

to the chair next to Gunnar's desk and had him sit. He hadn't done that for Perry's comfort but rather so he could get Laney away from the front windows. When she followed him, Owen motioned for her to go back toward the doorway to Kellan's office. She'd still be able to see and hear everything, but it might keep her out of harm's way.

"What you did was stupid," Kellan said, and he wasn't talking to Perry but rather to Emerson. "You confronted an armed man who could have killed you."

"I wasn't gonna kill anybody," Perry snapped.

Emerson came closer, practically toe-to-toe with Kellan. "You wouldn't stop him, so I did."

Nettie shook her head. "What's going on here? Why wouldn't you stop someone who was trying to blackmail my husband?"

"I didn't get a chance to stop him," Kellan assured her. "I only recently found out about the blackmail, and Emerson stormed out of here before giving me a chance to do anything about it."

They all looked at Gunnar when he came back in. He'd bagged a gun and was off his phone. "His name is Norman Perry. Age forty-three. He lives in San Antonio. No police record."

Now, that was another surprise. Owen would have thought the guy had a rap sheet. "Is the gun legal?" Owen asked Gunnar.

"I'll run it, but he's got a permit to carry concealed."

Another surprise, though Owen figured that people with permits could and did commit serious crimes. And this was indeed serious. Well, it was if Emerson had told the truth about the man.

"I took the classes for carrying concealed," Perry grumbled. "You've got no cause to hold me."

"He does," Emerson practically yelled. "He tried to blackmail me."

"No, I didn't." Not quite a shout from Perry, but it was close to one. "My girlfriend works for a company, Reliable Courier. She's sick, and her boss was swamped, so I said I'd make the delivery and do the pickup. That's all. Call Rick at Reliable Courier if you don't believe me."

This time, it was Kellan who made the call. While he did that, Owen continued with Perry, "Who hired Reliable Courier to meet with Emerson?"

"Wouldn't have a clue," Perry answered. "You'd have to ask Rick."

Owen was certain Kellan would do just that. "What were you supposed to pick up and deliver?"

Perry huffed, "Don't know that, either, but you can see for yourself on the delivery. The card is in a small envelope in my wallet. I put it there because it was little and I didn't want to lose it. My wallet's in the back pocket of my jeans."

Owen put on a pair of plastic gloves that Gunnar handed him. Without cutting off the restraints, Owen retrieved the wallet and pulled out a small envelope, the size that would be on a gift bouquet of flowers. There was a card inside, and someone had written what appeared to be the URL for a website. Beneath it was more writing labeled as a password.

"What is this?" Owen asked Perry.

"Hell if I know. Like I said, I'm just the deliveryman."

"He is," Kellan verified a moment later. He was still on his phone. "I'll check it all out, of course, but according to the owner, Perry was indeed just doing him a favor. He's getting me the client info now on the person who wanted this pickup and delivery."

Good. That might clear things up. Owen bagged the card and envelope, and Gunnar took it, first putting the official info on the bag and then taking it to the computer.

"Can I go now?" Perry complained.

"Not yet." Owen went to the computer to watch as Gunnar typed in the website, and Laney joined him. Nettie was still fussing over Emerson's injuries, but Emerson's attention was nailed to the monitor.

Gunnar entered the password, waited, and the images loaded on the screen. Photos.

"That's a photo of the safe-deposit box at the bank," Laney said, studying the image.

It was. Whoever had taken the picture had made sure the number was clearly visible.

Gunnar went to the next shot. A photo of the box open to show the manila envelope inside. Owen couldn't be sure, but it could have been the one from the photograph Terrance's PI had taken of Hadley the day she'd visited the bank.

"This is a hoax," Emerson said, and he hurried to Gunnar. Owen stepped in front of Emerson to stop him from doing whatever he'd been about to do. "Obviously this is just part of the blackmail scheme," Emerson insisted. "It'll be lies. All lies."

Owen wasn't sure about the lies part, but yeah, it was likely part of the blackmail. He held off Emerson while Gunnar loaded the next picture. It was a shot of photographs that appeared to have been removed from the manila envelope.

Photos of Emerson and Hadley.

"What is that?" Nettie asked. She moved closer, too, her gaze slashing from one image to the next.

"They're fake," Emerson growled, but the color had drained from his face, making that god-awful bruise stand out even more.

Owen didn't think so. There were two rows of photographs. The ones on the top row were semiselfies with Hadley awake and in bed, next to a sleeping Emerson. Since Emerson was on his back, it wasn't hard to miss that he was naked, and he certainly wasn't being restrained. His arms were stretched out like a sated man getting some rest.

The shots on the bottom row were ones that looked as if Hadley had taken them on the sly. Emerson in a glass shower and then while dressing. Owen couldn't tell if Emerson had been aware of the shots beings taken.

"They're fake," Emerson repeated, his voice wavering now.

Nettie didn't seem to hear him. She continued to study the photos.

"Rick at Reliable Courier got the name of the person who arranged for pickup and delivery," Kellan said. "He claimed his name was James Smith. The guy paid in cash, so I'm betting it's an alias."

Yeah. Owen figured that would prove to be true. He was also betting this James Smith was yet another hired gun. But why had the person who'd hired him left the blackmail to a courier company? That was something Owen needed to dig into.

Nettie shook her head. When she finally looked up at Emerson, there were tears in her eyes. She didn't have the distraught expression she'd had when she'd entered the sheriff's office. Now there was only hurt.

"You had sex with her," Nettie muttered. "Admit it. I want to hear you say it." Emerson reached for her, but she batted his hands away. "Say it!" This time her voice was a lot louder.

Emerson stared at her. And stared. "I had sex with her," he finally admitted. His gaze immediately flashed to Kellan. "But I didn't kill her."

The silence came, and it felt as if the entire room was holding its breath, waiting for whatever was about to happen.

Nettie finally broke that silence. "You lied," she said and, without even looking at Emerson, she headed for the door.

The first word that came to Owen's mind was *broken*. Nettie was broken.

"Wait!" Emerson called out as he rushed after her.

Nettie didn't stop. She just kept on walking, Emerson trailing along behind her.

"I'll go check on them," Gunnar said. "Should I bring them back inside?" he added to Kellan.

Kellan shook his head. "Not yet. Just make sure they aren't going to attack each other or anything. Then, once they've cooled off, I want Emerson back in here for questioning."

About a possible murder.

Hell. Owen groaned. Emerson had been denying this affair, but those pictures proved otherwise, which meant the man had been lying through his teeth.

But what else had he lied about?

Had Emerson actually been the one to kill Hadley?

Owen glanced at Laney, expecting to see some "I told you so" on her face, but there was none. There was only grief. No doubt because all of this had brought back the nightmarish memories of her sister's murder. She'd been right about Emerson lying about the affair, but sometimes being right didn't fix things.

"Emerson's not a flight risk," Kellan noted, "but I'll feel a lot better after Gunnar's brought him back in and I have him in the interview room."

Owen felt the same way.

"Can I go now?" Perry snapped.

Dragging in a frustrated breath, Kellan went to him and cut the restraints. "I'll need a statement first and then you can go." He tipped his head toward his office. "In there."

Only then did Owen remember they still had Terrance in the interview room, which was why Kellan hadn't sent Perry there.

"Let me get this website to the lab guys, and I'll talk to Terrance," Owen offered.

Owen started to do just that when his phone rang and he saw Eli's name on the screen. Since his brother was still at their grandparents' house with Addie and the others, Owen answered it right away.

"We got a problem," Eli immediately said. "One of the hands just spotted a gunman on the ranch."

Chapter Twelve

Everything inside Laney was racing. Her heart, her breath and the adrenaline. Just seconds before Eli's call, so many thoughts had been going through her head, but now there was only one.

Keep Addie safe.

Sweet heaven. The little girl had to be okay.

"Drive faster," Owen ordered his fellow deputy Raylene McNeal.

The deputy was behind the wheel of the cruiser with Owen and Laney in back. It had taken a stern, direct order from Kellan to stop Owen from driving, and Laney had been thankful for it. She figured his thoughts had to be racing even more than hers were.

Raylene mumbled something about already going too fast, but she sped up anyway. With the siren howling and the blue lights flashing, she raced down the road that led out of town and toward the ranch. At this speed, it wouldn't take long to get there, but every mile and every minute would feel like an eternity.

Owen had his gun drawn and had his phone gripped in his left hand. He no doubt wanted to be ready if Eli called him back with an update. And Eli would. But he obviously wouldn't be able to call if the ranch was under attack.

"You shouldn't have come," Owen said to her.

He'd already told her variations of that since they'd rushed out of the sheriff's office. Kellan hadn't issued her one of those stern orders but instead had given her a gun. It made sense. After all, she was a PI, knew how to shoot and Owen might need more backup than Kellan could provide. Still, Owen would see this as her being in danger again.

And he could be right.

But there was no chance she was going to stay back. Kellan had had no choice about that since someone needed to man the office, but Laney had had a choice. One she'd made despite Owen's objections.

Owen's phone dinged with a text, the sound piercing through the silence. "Gunnar's on his way to the ranch," he relayed when he read the message. "Kellan called him and pulled him off Emerson and Nettie."

Good. They might need all the help they could get. Plus, Emerson and Nettie might welcome the time to figure out how they were going to handle the bombshell of the affair. And then maybe Kellan could just go ahead and arrest him. Of course, Kellan would need some kind of evidence.

The photos were proof of an affair but not of murder.

Laney kept watch around them, knowing full well that the gunman at the ranch could be a ruse to get them on the road for another attack. But Laney didn't see anything, not even another vehicle.

The silence gave her mind a chance to stop racing, and maybe it was that temporary calm that allowed a fresh thought to creep into her head.

"Why would Hadley have taken those pictures?" Laney hadn't meant to say that aloud, but she had, and Owen had clearly heard it. Since he had, she continued, "She said he threatened her when he broke things off, but those photos were obviously taken when they were still together."

He glanced at her before he returned to keeping watch. "You think she was going to try to blackmail him?"

She shook her head. "Not for money. But maybe for emotional blackmail." Laney paused, forced herself to give that more thought. "Maybe Hadley thought she could use the pictures to force Emerson to stay with her."

Before Owen could respond, he got another text from Eli.

Gunman spotted just off the road leading to the ranch. Approach with caution. I'm in pursuit. Jack and one of the hands are in the house with Addie.

The road leading to the ranch was less than a mile away so Laney moved to the edge of her seat to try to spot him if and when he came into view.

"This had better not be a trap to lure Eli away from the house," Owen said under his breath.

And that sent her pulse into a full gallop. A gallop that was almost impossible for Laney to tamp down. "We're almost there," she reminded Owen, and in doing so, she reminded herself, so she could try to stay calm. "We need to keep an eye out for both the gunman and Eli."

Taking her own advice, Laney did just that while she kept a firm grip on her gun. Unfortunately, this stretch of the road was lined with fences, ditches and trees. Too many places for someone to hide. There was also another possibility: that the gunman had already driven off. It was possible he'd left a vehicle on the road, sneaked onto the ranch and, when he'd been spotted, could have run back to whatever transportation he'd used to get there.

"Kill the sirens," Owen told Raylene, and the deputy shut them off. No doubt so they'd be able to hear whatever was going on outside. Going in hot might drown out sounds that could lead them to the gunman's exact location.

Raylene slowed as she approached the turn for the ranch, and again Laney tried to pick through all the possible hiding places to spot or hear him. Nothing.

No sign of Eli, either, though she was certain he had to be somewhere in the area.

"There," Owen said, pointing toward the fence.

Laney immediately shifted her gaze in that direction, but she still didn't see anyone. Not at first anyway. And then she saw the blur of movement as someone darted between two trees.

"That's not Eli," Owen added.

No, it wasn't. Eli was tall and lanky, and this guy had bulky shoulders and a squat build. From the quick glimpse she'd gotten of him, Laney had thought he was armed with a rifle. That made sense because he could use it to fire from a distance. Heck, he could fire from this spot, depending on how good a scope he had. He likely wouldn't be able to fire into the grandparents' house, but the idiot could shoot at Eli.

Or at them.

And that was exactly what happened. Laney had no sooner had the thought when the bullet slammed into the window right where she was sitting. The safety glass shattered, but it held in place.

Cursing, Owen dragged her down onto the seat. Not a second too soon because three other shots blasted straight toward them, all hitting the glass. This time, it didn't hold, and the shards fell down onto them.

The sounds of the shots were still ringing in her ears, but Laney heard something else. Other rounds of gunfire, and these didn't seem to be coming from the shooter.

"Eli," Owen said. He kept her pushed down on the seat, but he levered up. Now that the glass had been knocked out, he took aim through the gaping hole.

He fired, too.

It was just a single shot, but it seemed to be enough because almost immediately she felt him relax just a little.

"The gunman's down," Raylene relayed.

Good. Laney didn't want the snake in any position to hurt Addie or anyone else. Maybe, though, he was still alive so he could give them answers.

"Pull up closer to Eli," Owen instructed Raylene. When the deputy did that, Owen moved off Laney. "Raylene, wait here with Laney," he said just seconds before he threw open the door.

Laney didn't get out with him, but she levered herself up so she could look out the window. She saw Owen running toward the man on the ground. Eli was also approaching him from the direction of the ranch. Owen reached the guy first and, after he kicked away the rifle, he reached down and touched his fingers to his neck. She didn't need to hear what the brothers said to each other to know that the shooter was indeed dead.

She heard the sounds of sirens. Gunnar. The cruiser was speeding up behind them, but as Raylene had done, Gunnar turned off the sirens as he came to a stop. The deputy barreled out of the car and ran toward Owen and Eli. Again, she couldn't hear what they said, but it didn't take long before Owen started quickly making his way back to Raylene and her.

When Owen got into the cruiser, he looked at Laney. Not just a glance, but more of an examination to make sure she hadn't been injured. She did the same to him. Thank goodness they hadn't been hurt. Not physically anyway. But this had put more shadows in his already dark eyes.

"Take us to my grandparents' house," Owen told Raylene.

Owen took hold of Laney, sliding her against him. Away from the glass and into his arms. For such a simple gesture, it did wonders. It steadied her heart enough that it no longer felt as if it might beat out of her chest. He didn't say anything but instead brushed his mouth on the top of her head. Another gesture that was anything but simple. It soothed her, aroused her and made her realize something.

She was falling in love with him.

Great. Just what she didn't need—and what Owen wouldn't want.

When Raylene pulled to a stop in front of his grandparents' house, she spotted two ranch hands, one on each side of the house. Jack opened the front door and, with his gun ready, stepped out onto the porch. No doubt to give them cover in case there were any snipers still around.

Owen didn't remind her that they'd have to move quickly. They did. Raylene, Owen and she all rushed out of the cruiser and into the house. The moment they were inside, Jack shut the door and rearmed the security system.

"I would ask if you're all okay," Jack said, "but I figure the answer to that is no. How about Eli?"

"He's with the dead gunman," Owen answered.

Jack gave an approving nod and tipped his head to the stairs. "Addie, Francine and Gemma are in the master bathroom. I told them to get into the bathtub and stay down."

Now it was Owen who gave a nod as he started up the stairs. Laney headed in that direction, too, but she stopped next to Jack. "I'm sorry."

He cocked an eyebrow. "I only want one apology and it's from the SOB who put all of this together. It took plenty of bucks to hire this many thugs to do these attacks and kill at least two people."

Yes, it did. "Both Terrance and Nettie have money like that."

"And Emerson," Jack quickly added. "No trust fund, but you can bet he could figure out a way to tap into his wife's money. Heck, Nettie's so much in love with him that she might have given him the cash with no questions asked."

All of that was true, and it was yet another reason for them to take a look at their financials.

Jack gave her a friendly, almost brotherly nudge on the arm before she tucked her loaner gun into the back waistband of her jeans and went up the stairs. She followed the sounds of the voices and found them still in the bath. Addie was in the giant tub, playing with a stash of toys, and Gemma, Francine and Owen were all sitting on the floor next to her.

The moment Laney stepped in, Addie looked at her and smiled. Like the way Owen had held her in the cruiser, that smile worked some magic.

"Horsey," Addie said, holding up one of her toys. It seemed to be an invitation for Laney to come closer. So she did, kneeling down beside the tub. Thankfully, the little girl didn't seem to be aware that she was in this room because there had been another attack.

"You think it's okay for me to go to the kitchen?" Francine asked Owen.

He nodded. "Just stay away from the windows."

Francine thanked him as she got to her feet. "I think I need a cup of tea."

"I need a drink," Gemma added, getting up, as well. "A strong one with lots of booze, and then I'm going to call Kellan."

Laney nearly told the women there was no reason to leave on her account, but she realized she wanted this time with Owen and Addie. Even if it was for only a few seconds.

Gemma gave her arm a gentle squeeze, a show of support, which Laney greatly appreciated.

After the women were gone, Laney brushed her hand over the tips of Addie's curly hair and got another smile from the little girl. Laney found herself smiling, too. Yes, this was definitely magic.

"I'll go into the other bedroom so you can be with her," Laney told him, but when she started to stand, Owen took hold of her hand and kept her in place. He didn't say anything. He just kept his grip on her while he continued to watch his daughter.

"I've been thinking about setting up a safe house and moving Addie there," Owen finally told her long moments later.

That didn't surprise her, not with the repeated attacks, but Laney thought she knew why that had put such an unsettled look on Owen's already troubled face. "You wouldn't be able to go with her."

"No. I'd need to be here, to see this investigation through to an arrest. Plus, it might be a good idea to put some distance between her and me."

"Distance between Addie and *me*," Laney corrected. She sighed, groaned. "I'm the target."

Owen quickly shook his head and caught her chin to force eye contact. "Maybe you were the sole target in the beginning, but those shots have been fired at me, too."

"They wouldn't be if you weren't with me," she pointed out just as fast.

Now he was the one to sigh, and he stared at her a long time before he said anything else. "So far, the attacks have happened when we were outside, and the hired thugs haven't managed to get close enough to this house to fire any shots inside."

That was true, but she was about to argue that it could change, that this latest gunman might be the first in a string of others to come. But she could see the risk of taking the baby out on the road—even in a cruiser. Yes, a cruiser was bullet-resistant, but shots could get through. They'd just had proof of that.

"The ranch hands are willing to keep guarding the place?" she asked.

Owen nodded. "I suspect Jack will have to leave. Raylene, too. But Eli and I can stay here. And we have you for backup."

That was more than just a little vote of confidence. It actually caused some of the tightness in Laney's chest to go away. Owen trusted her to be part of this.

"Thanks," she managed to say, half expecting him to ask why she'd said that.

He didn't. Owen reached out, sliding his fingers over her jaw. To her cheek. And then to the back of her neck. He leaned in slowly. So slowly. Until his mouth brushed over hers. Almost immediately, he pulled back, their gazes connecting. A dozen things passed between them. Unspoken words but they still understood.

The need.

The ache.

The impossibility of it all.

Laney felt every one of those things, in every inch of her, and she was certain Owen did, too.

"Kissy," Addie said, clapping.

The moment between Laney and Owen was gone, replaced by another one that seemed even more important. And possible. Using the side of the tub, Addie got to her feet and dropped a kiss on Owen's cheek before doing the same to Laney.

"Kissy," Addie repeated, beaming with that incredible smile.

Yes, this was more important.

Owen scooped Addie out of the tub and into his lap and showered her with loud kisses that had the little girl giggling. Addie leaned over and spread some of those giggles and kisses to Laney, including her in a moment that she didn't deserve to share. But it was a moment that she'd never forget.

It didn't last, though. Owen's phone rang and even though Addie was only a toddler, she seemed to understand the importance of it because she moved into Laney's lap when Owen took out his phone. Laney saw Kellan's name on the screen, which was probably why Owen didn't put the call on speaker. Not with Addie right there. He wouldn't want to risk her hearing anything about the dead gunman.

To make sure Addie was spared that, Laney got up and shifted the little girl onto her hip so they could go out into the adjoining bedroom. Keeping hold of her hands, she let Addie jump on the bed, something that Francine had let her do. Of course, that seemed like a lifetime ago.

Everything did.

She'd come here, lying, looking for Hadley's killer. That had seemed the most important thing in the world. In some ways, it still was. But now it wasn't just about finding justice, it was about putting an end to the danger so that this precious little girl, Owen and his family would be safe.

Laney pulled Addie back into her arms when Owen entered the room, and she could tell from his expression that he'd just gotten more bad news.

"Rohan Gilley's lawyer just visited him at the sheriff's office, and after he left, Gilley told Kellan that he was finally ready to talk," Owen explained.

She shook her head, not understanding his somber tone, because it was good that the hired gun had broken his silence. "And?" Laney prompted when Owen didn't add anything.

Owen dragged in a breath through his mouth. "Gilley said that Emerson is the one who hired him."

Chapter Thirteen

Emerson.

Owen had already cursed his brother-in-law, but he kept cursing under his breath every time his calls to Emerson went to voice mail. Where the hell was he? Since Nettie wasn't answering her phone, either, Owen could only guess that Emerson had gotten wind of Gilley's "confession" and had gone on the run.

To avoid being arrested for murder.

That only caused Owen to silently swear even more, and the profanity wasn't just aimed at Emerson. He aimed plenty at himself. All the signs had been there, and Laney had said right from the get-go that Emerson had killed her sister. He hadn't listened and now they were in this mess.

"No one in Emerson's office has seen him," Eli relayed when he finished his latest round of calls.

Eli and Owen were only two of the people looking for Emerson. Gunnar and Raylene were back at the sheriff's office. Kellan was no doubt doing it, too, though he likely had his hands full with Gilley and getting the warrant not just for Emerson but for his financials. Because he'd been swamped and since there'd been no evidence to hold him, Kellan had cut Terrance loose. Temporarily anyway. Terrance would be making a return trip to the sheriff's office for further questioning. That might not even be necessary, though. If they could arrest Emerson and get him in the box for questioning, he might confess all.

Might.

And he might deny it, just as he'd denied the affair with Hadley. At least, he'd denied it until he'd had to face those pictures.

"I'm sure it's occurred to you that Gilley could be lying through his teeth," Eli pointed out.

Owen nodded. Yeah. In fact, that had been his first thought. After all, Gilley wasn't exactly a responsible, law-abiding citizen. He could have simply grown tired of being in a cell, waiting for a plea deal, and had decided to strike out.

"If there'd been no circumstantial evidence against Emerson, Kellan probably wouldn't have even told me what Gilley had said," Owen answered. "But there is evidence."

Eli made a sound of agreement. "And it doesn't help that he's gone AWOL. If that's what happened."

Owen looked at his brother, who was at the living

room window. "You think something could have happened to him?"

"Depends on if he's really a killer or not. If it's Nettie or Terrance, then Emerson could be the next victim. They might try to make it look like a suicide."

Owen could definitely see that happening, but maybe before anyone else died, Emerson would come in and give a statement.

"You should get some rest," Eli added when Owen groaned and rubbed his eyes. "I'll be fine to keep first watch. Better yet, why don't you make sure Laney is okay?"

Eli took something from his pocket and tossed it to Owen. Only after Owen caught it did he realize what it was. A foil-wrapped condom.

Owen scowled at him.

"You think you'll need two of them?" Eli asked in his best smart-mouthed tone.

Owen scowled some more. But he slipped the condom into his pocket, causing Eli to smile. It made Owen want to punch him. Or thank him. Before he could decide which, he turned and made his way up the stairs.

He checked on Addie first and saw that she was sacked out in her crib. Francine and Gemma had taken the bed and were asleep, too. Only then did he remember he'd told them that he'd likely be getting up in the middle of the night for watch duty. Obviously the women had decided to make that easy for him by switching around the sleeping arrangements.

Owen checked on Laney next because he hadn't had a chance to talk to her since the Gilley bombshell about Emerson. And no, "checking on" her didn't have anything to do with the condom.

Probably not anyway.

Her door was open, but his heart dropped to his knees when he didn't see her inside. A few seconds later, she came out of the hall bathroom. She was wearing a robe several sizes too big for her and was toweling her wet hair.

"Emerson?" she immediately asked, and her whispered voice hardly had any sound.

He shook his head, saw the mixture of disappointment and frustration go over her face, but she didn't say anything else until they were in the bedroom. "Emerson might not be guilty."

Since that was the same conversation he'd just had with Eli and then with himself, Owen nodded and shut the door so they wouldn't wake Addie, Francine or Gemma.

"Gut feeling?" he asked.

"Just trying to give him the benefit of the doubt. I want the attacks to stop, but I want to make sure the right person pays for that." She paused. "Even if Emerson killed Hadley, it doesn't mean he hired those thugs."

Owen believed that, too. That, of course, put them right back to not having a clear suspect.

He stayed by the door while she continued to dry her hair and pace. Owen figured she wouldn't be getting a lot of sleep tonight, either. However, when the towel shifted a little, that was when he saw the cut on her right temple.

"You're hurt?" he asked, going to her.

"No. It's only a little cut."

He didn't have to ask how she'd gotten it. It'd been when the gunman had shot through the glass. He hadn't seen it earlier because her hair had covered her.

No, she wouldn't be getting any sleep tonight.

She looked at him, forced a smile. "You do know it's not a good idea for you to be in here, right?" she asked.

"I know." He didn't hesitate, either, and had no doubts about that. It was a *very bad* idea.

But he didn't budge.

There was a storm stirring inside him, and it spread until he thought there wasn't any part of him not affected by it. All fire, and it was edged with danger. He thought maybe if he'd been facing down gunmen, it wouldn't have felt as strong as this.

Laney must have sensed that storm because her breath kicked up a notch. It was heavy, causing her chest to rise and fall as if she'd just run a long distance. He saw the pulse on her throat. Took in her scent, something beneath the soap she'd used in the shower.

Her scent.

It roared through him even faster than the storm.

He had a dozen arguments with himself as to why he should turn around and leave. And, one by one, he lost every one of those debates. Because right now there was only one thing that mattered. One thing that he knew he had to have.

Laney.

Owen went to her, pulled her into arms and started what he was certain he would regret soon enough. He kissed her.

FROM THE MOMENT she'd stepped from her shower and had seen Owen, Laney had figured it would lead to this kiss. She hadn't seen any way around it. That didn't make it right.

No. Owen would almost certainly feel guilty about this. Once the heat had cooled down, he would consider it a lapse in judgment. But she wouldn't. She would see it as her one chance to be with him.

And she would take it.

Even if Owen wasn't hers to take.

Laney melted into his arms, into the kiss. It wasn't hard to do. She wanted him more than she wanted her next breath, and with that clever kiss, he was giving her everything she needed. The taste of him. The fit of her body in his arms. The feel of his mouth on

hers. And she got even more of that when he deepened the kiss.

Both his mouth and hands were rough. Rushed.
Maybe from the same fiery need she was feeling
or because he didn't want to pause long enough to
change his mind. But Laney made him pause. She
pulled back, met his gaze, looked straight into those
storm-gray eyes. She didn't say a word. Didn't have
to. She just gave him those seconds to reconsider.

Their gazes held. So deep. So long. And it wasn't
necessary for them to have a conversation. He told
her all she needed to know when his mouth came
back to hers. Owen snapped her against him, his
hand slipping into her robe and pushing open the
sides.

She was naked beneath, something he soon dis-
covered when his fingers brushed over her nipple.
He still didn't stop. Didn't even hesitate when he
lowered his head and took her nipple into his mouth.

The fire shot through her, flooding the heat to the
center of her body. Oh, she wanted him.

Owen didn't stop with the breast kiss. He trailed
his mouth, and tongue, lower to her stomach. He
might have gone even lower if she hadn't stopped
him and pulled him back up.

"You're wearing too many clothes," she protested
and immediately tried to do something about that.

She fumbled with the buttons on his shirt and then
cursed his shoulder harness when she couldn't get

it off him. Owen helped with that, kissing her and backing her across the room. At first, she couldn't figure out why he wasn't taking her to the bed, but then Laney realized he'd locked the door.

Good grief. Anyone could have walked in on them, and his daughter was just across the hall. That reminder gave her a moment's pause that might have lasted longer if Owen's next kiss hadn't sent her back into the melting mode. Mercy. The man could kiss.

And touch.

Yes, she soon learned he was very clever at that, too. With his hands skimming along her body, he moved her toward the bed, easing her back on the mattress while his fingers found their way between her legs.

The touch took her breath away and caused the pleasure to spear through her. But soon, very soon, it wasn't nearly enough. She wanted him, all of him, and that started with getting him naked.

"Still too many clothes," she complained. "Get them off now."

That finally spurred him to a different kind of action and, while still kissing her, he shucked off his shirt. Laney finally got her chance to touch him. His chest was toned and perfect like the rest of him. She ran her hand down to his jeans to get his belt undone.

And she unzipped him.

She gave in to the heat from the kisses and touched him, sliding her hand into his boxers. Touching him.

A sound came deep from his throat. Part groan, part pleasure. She saw urgency come to his eyes. Felt it when he shoved his hand in his jeans pocket and took out a condom.

Laney pushed off his jeans and boots as he put on the condom. Both ate up seconds and caused the pressure to soar. *Now*, she kept repeating in her mind. *Now.*

Owen gave her now.

With the fire and need consuming them, he pushed into her and she closed around him. Owen stilled for a moment, his eyes coming back to hers. More long moments. But these seemed...necessary. As if they both had to know that this wasn't ordinary. That it wasn't just the heat. No. It was a lot more than that, whether they wanted it to be or not.

He was breathing through his mouth now. Heavy, sharp gusts. But still, his eyes—dark and heavy— moved over her, taking her into his mind just as she'd taken him into her body.

When he started to move, he did it slowly. Long, easy strokes. Stretching out the pleasure. That didn't last, either.

Couldn't.

The urgency returned with a vengeance. Something primal that was bone-deep. His need to finish this. The strokes came faster. Deepened. Kept pace with her quick, throbbing pulse. The need came faster, too. Demanding that now, now, now.

Owen gave her that, too.

He pushed into her until the climax slammed through her. Her vision pinpointed just him before it blurred. Before the only thing she could do was hold on. And take him with her.

Chapter Fourteen

When Owen came back from the bathroom, he'd expected to find Laney already dressed and either pacing or working on the laptop. But she was still naked and apparently asleep. She was on her stomach, her hand tucked like a pillow beneath her face. She looked…well, peaceful.

And beautiful.

No way would he convince his body otherwise. Not a chance of convincing it—or rather, certain parts of him anyway—that he didn't want her all over again. That wouldn't have been such a bad thing if one of those parts hadn't been his heart.

Hell.

He hadn't just had sex with her. He'd made love to her. Big difference, and he was honest enough with himself to not try to downplay it. Sex was easy, often with no strings or ones that didn't matter. But there'd be important strings with Laney. Not from her. He was guessing she'd give him an out and say that it didn't matter. She wouldn't be doing that for herself but rather for him.

Owen wouldn't take an out. He'd never been the sort to dismiss his feelings, which meant he was going to have to somehow work out this guilt going through him about Naomi. In a way, it felt as if he'd cheated on her. Or worse, it felt as if he'd finally gotten past her death. And that was worse than the guilt.

Pulling in a long breath, he eased down next to Laney on the bed. She automatically moved closer to him, draping her arm over his chest, and he felt the muscles tense in her arm. She opened one eye, looked at him and frowned.

"You're dressed." She started to scramble away from him, probably to put on her clothes, but he dragged her against him, holding her.

She didn't move away, but she did look up at him. He recognized suspicion in a person's eyes when he saw it. Suspicion. Then lust. She glanced at the door, probably to see if he'd shut it. He had.

"I'm naked," she said. "You're not. I think this would probably work better if you were naked, too."

That made him smile, and Owen brushed a kiss on the top of her head. He just wanted a moment, with her like this in his arms. It didn't settle the guilt trip in his mind, but it sure as heck settled the rest of him.

She levered herself up, touched her fingers to the bunched-up part of his forehead. "What is it?" she asked.

Owen wasn't sure he would have told her, but he didn't get the chance to decide because his phone buzzed. He'd turned off the ringer so that it wouldn't wake Addie, Francine or Gemma, but the buzz came through loud and clear.

Emerson's name was on the screen.

"Put it on speaker," Laney insisted as she got to her feet and began to dress.

Owen did, but he turned down the volume. "Where are you?" Owen immediately asked.

"I'm driving to the ranch. We need to talk."

Yeah, they definitely needed to talk, but Owen didn't want Emerson within a mile of the ranch. "Go to the sheriff's office. Kellan's there and he'll talk to you."

Emerson made a sound of outrage. "You're my brother-in-law, not Kellan. I want to talk to you."

"The hands have orders not to let anyone on the ranch." Owen spelled it out for him. "They won't let you on."

Emerson cursed. "Didn't you hear what I said? We need to talk. I can't find Nettie, and I think someone's trying to kill me."

Owen didn't say "Welcome to the club," but that was what he was thinking. Laney, too, because she rolled her eyes. "What makes you think someone's trying to kill you?" Owen prompted.

"Because a car's been following me. I've got a

gun, but if these are hired killers, they'll be a lot better shot than I am."

"Funny you should mention that. Rohan Gilley, the gun we have in custody, said you were his boss."

That brought on a whole new round of cursing from Emerson. "He's a lying SOB. I didn't hire him. I haven't done anything wrong."

"Nothing other than lying to keep your affair with Hadley a secret," Owen reminded him.

"I didn't kill her!" Emerson shouted. "I didn't kill anyone, and I sure as hell didn't hire Rohan Gilley."

Owen had no idea if that were true, but even if he believed him, he wouldn't let Emerson on the ranch. They were on lockdown, and it was going to stay that way until they were no longer in danger.

"Go to the sheriff's office," Owen repeated. "Give your statement to Kellan. If there's someone following you, someone who intends to do you harm, then Kellan can also put you in protective custody."

"Is that where Nettie went?" Emerson snapped.

Owen didn't have a clue, but since that might urge Emerson to go there, he settled for saying, "Could be. You should check and see. And do it soon, Emerson," Owen added just as the man ended the call.

He had no idea if his brother-in-law would actually do that, but maybe he would so they could begin to start putting together the pieces of this puzzle.

By the time Owen put his phone away, Laney was completely dressed. Something that didn't please the nonheart part of him. He considered getting her out of those clothes again and going for another round, but he didn't have a second condom and wouldn't ask Eli for one.

Well, maybe he wouldn't.

Owen was pretty sure the moment Eli saw his face, his brother would be able to figure out what had gone on. Heck, Eli might even volunteer another condom then—even though the timing sucked. Owen mentally repeated that part about the timing, got up and faced Laney.

"I'm going down to relieve Eli for a while," he said.

"I'll go with you and grab something to eat."

Until she'd added that last part, Owen had been about to tell her to get some rest, but since she hadn't eaten anything all day, he didn't want to nix a good idea. He might even be able to grab a bite, as well.

Apparently, good sex spurred the appetite.

Owen peeked in again on Addie before Laney and he made their way down the stairs. And yep, Eli did figure it out. The corner of Eli's mouth lifted in a smile, but he thankfully dropped the expression when Laney came in. She greeted Eli and went straight into the adjoining kitchen.

"Don't say a word," Owen warned Eli.

Eli didn't, but he did chuckle. If it was loud enough for Laney to hear, she didn't react. She started making sandwiches from some cold cuts that she took from the fridge.

"Why don't you get some sleep?" Owen suggested.

"Will do after I fix me one of those sandwiches." Eli traded places with him, and Owen moved to the window as his brother went into the kitchen with Laney.

It was dark outside. No moon. But there were security lights on the road leading to the house. Owen had debated as to whether or not to turn them off. Debated keeping off all the lights inside, too, so that no one would easily be able to see they were there. However, he'd nixed the idea since the security lights would make it easier for the hands to see if someone tried to get onto the ranch.

Owen was less than a minute into his watch duties when his phone buzzed again. He silently cursed, figuring it was Emerson. But no, it was Terrance. Owen answered, putting the call on speaker because both Laney and Eli had entered the room, no doubt to listen.

"Are you at the sheriff's office?" Terrance asked, continuing before he gave Owen a chance to answer. "Because I need to see you."

"I'm a popular man tonight," Owen grumbled. "What do you want?"

Considering Terrance had blurted the first part of his conversation, it surprised Owen when the man went silent. Owen was about to repeat his "what do you want" demand when Terrance finally spoke.

"Look, I need to explain some things, that's all." Terrance definitely didn't sound like his usual cocky self. "Your brother, the sheriff, made it clear that he's looking at me for Nancy's murder."

"Yeah, because she worked for you," Owen was quick to remind him.

"She did, but I swear I didn't have anything to do with her murder."

That was the second time tonight that someone had denied being a killer. Owen wasn't any more inclined to believe him than he was Emerson.

"I didn't kill Nancy," Terrance went on. And he paused again. "But she did get into that bank box to get the pictures."

Laney dropped the bag of chips she'd taken from the cabinet and hurried closer to Owen. Eli moved closer, too, eating his sandwich. While he wasn't hurrying, it was obvious his attention was nailed to the conversation.

"I'm listening," Owen told Terrance.

"Once I made the connection between Hadley and a safe-deposit box, I wanted to know what was inside," Terrance admitted.

Owen's jaw tightened. "Why? Because you thought there was some kind of evidence in there that would get your conviction overturned?" And yes, that question was loaded with sarcasm.

"No. I was guilty of assaulting Laney, and I served my time," he quickly added. "I just thought there might be something that would…punish Laney. Something to give her a dose of the same pain she gave me when she didn't do her job and vet the gold digger who drained me dry."

Owen was about to point out that Terrance had been the one stupid enough to fall for a con artist, but Laney spoke before Owen could.

"Punish me?" Laney repeated. "How?"

Terrance muttered some profanity. "I thought it would bring back bad memories for you. Something that would make you feel guilty for not finding your sister's killer." He paused. "When I told Nancy this, she took it upon herself to get into the bank. I never hired her to do that, never encouraged her."

Owen doubted that. There'd likely been plenty of *encouragement*. Payment, too.

"How'd Nancy get the key to the box?" Owen queried.

"I'm not sure. She didn't tell me."

Owen doubted that, as well. There was a slim chance that Nancy could have bribed someone at the bank to get her a duplicate key. Also a slim chance that Nancy had killed Joe and got the key from him. But all of this pointed straight back to Terrance.

"Nancy acted of her own accord," Terrance declared. "Because she thought it would be a favor to me."

"A favor?" Owen challenged. "She committed a felony. This is more than just a favor."

Terrance made a sound of agreement. "She had a thing for me and probably thought I'd be so grateful that it'd start up something personal between us. It didn't."

Owen would give that some more thought later, but for now he wanted to keep pressing for details. Then he could sort out what were lies and what were truths.

"What happened when Nancy went to the bank?" Owen asked.

"She called and said the only thing in the box was a bunch of pictures. Pictures of Hadley and the married DA. I wasn't sure how I could use those, but I told her to copy them, put them in online storage and then put the originals in a safe place."

"And then you killed Nancy?" Owen finished for him.

"No! Of course not." There was plenty of emotion in his voice now and some of it sounded like regret. "Nancy asked if she could make some money off the pictures, maybe by getting the DA to buy them. I told her no, that I didn't want her to do that." Another pause. "But I think she tried. I think that's what got her killed."

Yeah, maybe killed by Terrance himself because the woman had disobeyed his order. "Who murdered Nancy?" Owen demanded.

"I don't know, but I refuse to be blamed for her death. I won't let your brother come after me and try to stick me behind bars." The anger was back with a vengeance, and his voice started to rise. "I won't go back to jail."

"You won't have a choice about that. If there's any proof whatsoever that you paid Nancy to go to the bank—"

"There isn't," Terrance interrupted. "Because I'm innocent, and as far as I'm concerned, this will be the last conversation I have with Laney, your brother or you." With that, Terrance ended the call.

Owen wasn't so sure about this being the last, but he hoped that Terrance would truly stay out of Laney's life. That would definitely happen if Terrance was arrested for murder.

"If Terrance was telling the truth about Nancy," Laney said, "maybe the woman used the courier so she'd be one step removed from the blackmail. In fact, she could have paid someone to contact the courier service."

As theories went, it wasn't a bad one, and if that was what happened, then Terrance could indeed be innocent. But that left them with the same question he'd just presented to Terrance. Who killed Nancy?

Eli was still chowing down on his sandwich when his phone buzzed. "It's Jeremy," he relayed to them. Jeremy Cranston, one of the ranch hands. Eli took the call on speaker.

"I just spotted someone in the back pasture," Jeremy said. "A man. And he's got a rifle."

LANEY'S STOMACH TIGHTENED into a cold, hard knot, and she realized this was something she had been expecting. Something she'd prayed wouldn't happen.

But here it was.

"The armed guy isn't close to the house," Jeremy added a moment later. "I saw him through the binoculars as he came over the fence. Should I leave Bennie here and head out to that part of the pasture?" Laney knew that Bennie Deavers was the other ranch hand helping them guard the immediate area around the house.

"No," Owen answered. "Just keep an eye on the intruder. He could be a lure to get us to go after him."

Oh, God. She hadn't even considered that. She should have, though. Laney should have anticipated that whoever was behind this would do anything to get to her.

But why?

She still didn't know, and that tore away at her as much as the fear for Owen, his family and the hands.

"Have you seen anyone else?" Owen asked Jeremy. "Maybe somebody on the road?"

"Nobody. Don't have to tell you, though, that there are a lot of acres. A lot of ways for someone to get here if they're hell-bent on it."

No, Jeremy didn't have to tell them. And yes, the person after her was definitely hell-bent.

She thought of all the old trails that coiled around the ranch and fed out into the roads. Once they'd been used to move cattle and equipment before the roads had been built. Now they could provide access to someone who wanted to get close without being seen.

"Keep an eye on all sides of the house," Owen instructed as he turned off the lights. Eli went into the living room and did the same. "Just keep an eye on the gunman and text Eli or me when he gets closer to the house."

Eli had already moved to the front window to keep watch when he ended the call. Owen moved to the kitchen window, but he looked at Laney.

"Have Francine and Gemma move Addie into the tub," he said. "You go in the bathroom with them."

"Yes to the first. No to the second," Laney argued. "You need backup, and I not only have a gun, I know how to use it."

Laney didn't give him a chance to answer. She ran up the stairs to get Addie to safety. Gemma must have heard her coming because the woman stepped out into the hall.

"There's an armed man in the pasture" was all Laney said, and Gemma hurried back into the room to scoop up Addie.

"Francine, get up," Gemma insisted, already heading to the adjoining bathroom. Thankfully, Addie didn't wake up, and Laney hoped it stayed that way.

The nanny sprang off the bed, her eyes wide with fear. Fear that Laney couldn't soothe because the danger had returned. "I'll come back up when the threat is over," Laney assured her. She prayed that wouldn't be too long.

Of course, after this threat was over, Owen would no doubt make the decision to move Addie. This was the second intruder in only a handful of hours, and he had to get his daughter out of harm's way. That meant taking the little girl to a safe house—away from Owen. And Owen would almost certainly insist that Laney go into a safe house, as well. Not with Addie, though. No. The best way to protect Addie was to get her away from Laney.

Once Francine and Gemma had Addie in the bathroom, Laney made sure all the upstairs lights were off and then hurried downstairs. Since Owen was still in the kitchen and Eli at the front of the living room, Laney went to the side window positioned between the two areas. They could cover three sides of the house in case this armed thug got past the ranch hands.

And the wait began.

It was impossible for Laney to tamp down all the fear that was rising inside her. Impossible to keep her breathing and heartbeat level. But she forced herself to remember her training. She didn't have nearly the level of expertise that Owen and Eli did, but she'd taken self-defense and firearms classes. Maybe, though, it wouldn't come down to any of them using those skills.

The room was so quiet that Laney nearly gasped when she heard the sound. Not an intruder. It was Eli's phone that dinged with a text message.

Volleying glances between the window and his phone, Eli read it. Then he cursed. "Jeremy said he lost sight of the armed idiot and thinks the guy went behind the trees."

Laney wanted to curse, too. That definitely hadn't been what she'd wanted to hear. Now the guy could be anywhere, including much too close to the house.

"Keep watch," Eli reminded them as he slipped his phone back into his pocket.

She did. Laney's gaze went from one side of her area to the other. Trees, yes. A white rail fence. And she could see the edge of the barn behind the house. What she couldn't see were any signs of a hired gun. Since Owen had a much better view of the barn, she glanced at him just as he glanced at her. And he shook his head.

"Nothing that I can see," he said.

"How's the security system rigged?" she asked. She was certain that Owen had already mentioned it, but she wanted to make sure.

"There are alarms on all windows and doors,

including the windows on the top floor. If anyone tries to get in, we'll know about it."

Good. It was especially good about the alarms being on the second story of the house. Laney doubted the intruder could get a ladder past the ranch hands, but even if by some miracle that happened, he wouldn't be able to just break in without alerting them.

Her heart skipped a couple of beats when she saw something move by the barn, and Laney automatically pivoted in that direction. It got Eli and Owen's attention, and she heard them shift their positions, too. Then she saw the yellow tabby cat skirt out from the barn and dart across the yard.

"It was just the cat," Laney said. Even though she couldn't actually hear Eli and Owen take breaths of relief, she figured that was what they were doing. She certainly was.

Eli's phone dinged again, putting her heart in her throat as she waited for him to relay the text. "Jeremy caught sight of him by the left side of the barn."

The barn. Much too close. And possibly the reason the cat had run.

She couldn't see the left side of the barn from her position, so she shifted, moving to the other side of the window. She still didn't have a clear view, but she could see more of the barn.

As she'd done earlier, Laney took aim in that direction. Just as she heard another sound. One she didn't want to hear.

A gunshot.

OWEN SAW THE rifle a split second before the bullet crashed through the kitchen window right next to where he was standing.

Almost immediately the security alarm went off, the shrill, clanging sounds pulsing through the house. The bullet had been loud, deafening even, but the alarms were drowning out sounds that he wanted to hear.

Like any kind of movement in the yard.

If this armed thug was coming closer to the house, Owen darn sure wanted to know about it. Plus, he needed to make sure Francine and Gemma weren't calling out for help.

"Kill the alarm," Owen shouted to Eli.

His brother was closer to the keypad by the door, and besides, the shooter was obviously at the back of the house, where Owen was.

Using the wall as cover, Owen glanced around the window frame at the barn. He didn't see anything, but he knew the guy was there, hiding in the shadows. Waiting to do some more damage. He got proof of that when he saw the rifle again.

Owen immediately fired, but the shooter must not have been hit because he managed to get off a shot. A second bullet came crashing through what was left of the window. The guy fired a third shot, then a fourth, but Owen couldn't tell where the last two had landed.

He prayed they hadn't gone upstairs.

Just the thought sent his heart and fear into overdrive. He knew that Francine would have Addie in the tub where she'd be relatively safe, but he didn't want *relatively* when it came to his daughter. He wanted this idiot gunman dead so he couldn't send any more lethal shots anywhere near the house.

The house went silent when Eli turned off the alarm, and Owen immediately listened for Francine. Nothing, thank God. And he added another thanks when he didn't hear Addie crying.

"I've reset the security system," his brother said. "But I had to turn off the sensors on the windows. *All* the windows," Eli emphasized. "It was the only way to shut off the alarms."

That wasn't ideal, but at least the doors would still be armed, and if the gunman came through a window, he'd have to break the glass since they were all locked. Owen knew that because he'd checked them all himself.

With his attention still on the barn, Owen heard the dinging sound of a text message from Eli's phone.

"Jeremy's been hit in the leg," Eli relayed, tacking on some raw curse words. "Bennie says it's not bad, and he's tying off the wound."

Good. Owen definitely didn't want the hand

dying, but the injury basically took out both men who'd been guarding the house. It pinned them down so they might not be able to shoot the gunman even if they caught sight of him.

"Should I call for backup?" Laney asked.

Owen purposely hadn't looked at her—because he hadn't wanted to remember that she, too, was in danger, but he glanced at her now and shook his head. "I don't want anyone else coming into an ambush."

In fact, he wanted her away from the window, but the truth was, with the hands out of commission, Owen needed her eyes and gun right now. Laney seemed ready to give them both. She certainly didn't look as if she might fall apart. Just the opposite. She had a firm grip on her weapon and had it aimed in the direction of the barn.

"I'll call Kellan and an ambulance," Eli volunteered. "But I will tell them to hold off, to keep some distance from the house. I agree. I don't want anyone else gunned down tonight."

Owen listened while his brother made the quick call. That would put Kellan and the EMTs on standby at least, and he hoped like the devil that no one else got hurt. Well, no one other than the idiot who'd shot Jeremy.

He dragged in a hard breath and held it while he continued to take glances out at the barn. He couldn't wait long, though. Despite having Bennie there to help, Jeremy would soon need medical attention.

Besides, Owen couldn't have any more shots being fired into the house.

"I see him," Laney blurted. Before Owen could even respond, she fired, her shot blasting through the window. The glass practically exploded from the impact.

Laney ducked back. Barely in the nick of time because the gunman returned fire, sending a shot right at her. This one didn't just take out more glass but also a chunk of wood from the window frame. A reminder that those bullets could go through the walls.

Owen saw the blood on Laney's face. No doubt a cut from the flying glass or wood. And it turned his stomach. She was hurt, and even though it was probably minor, he hated that this snake had been able to get to her. Hated even more that the injury could have been much worse.

Laney didn't even react to the cut. She adjusted her position again, still staying by the window, and Owen quit glancing at her so that he could keep his attention nailed to the barn.

The seconds crawled by as he waited, his finger on the trigger. He knew that Eli and Laney were doing the same thing, but Owen didn't hear or see anything.

When the seconds turned to minutes, Owen knew he had to do something. Jeremy needed help, and they couldn't just stand there. He was going to have to do something to draw out the gunman.

"Eli, keep low but come back here," Owen instructed. "I'm going to duck out from cover. When he takes aim at me, shoot him."

"No," Laney insisted. "You could be shot."

Yeah. But so could everybody else in the house. Owen didn't say that to her, though. He just waited until Eli was in position on the other side of the window. Owen gave him the nod and leaned out from cover.

Nothing.

No rifle barrel. No gunman.

Where the hell was he? Owen was about to ask Eli to text Jeremy to see if he had eyes on the gunman, but before he could do that, Owen heard something that shot fresh adrenaline through him.

The alarm from the security system.

Someone had tripped it, and that someone was in the house.

Chapter Fifteen

Laney tried to tamp down the jolt of fear she got from the alarm, but it was impossible not to react.

The gunman was almost certainly inside.

She forced her mind to clear so she could do a quick review of the house. Eli had said the windows were no longer armed so the intruder must have come in through a door.

Laney could see both the front door in the foyer and the back door in the kitchen. They were closed, so that left two other points of entry. The one at the side of the house off the family room. Or the one that led from carport area and into the house. Either one of those could give him access to the kitchen.

Or the back stairs that led to the second floor.

"Addie," Owen said over the clamor of the alarm.

Eli nodded. "I'll go up and guard the door." She saw the same fear and concern in his eyes that was no doubt in hers.

Eli had likely volunteered because he was closer,

right at the base of the front stairs. Without waiting for Owen's response, he disengaged the security system, silencing the alarms again, then barreled up the steps, taking them two at a time.

Owen hurried into the living room with her, positioning them so they were back to back. He didn't have to tell her to keep watch of the foyer in case the gunman came that way. He did the same to the back of the house.

Even with the silenced alarm, it was still hard for Laney to hear, but she picked her way through her throbbing pulse so she could listen. Nothing. Not at first. And then she heard what she was sure was someone moving around.

Owen must have heard it, too, because the muscles in his body stiffened even more than they already were. "It came from the family room," he whispered, automatically switching places with her so that he faced that direction.

Laney didn't like that he'd done that to take her out of the line of fire, but she knew that was an argument she wouldn't win. No way would Owen just stand there and let her face danger when he could do something about it.

Owen cursed softly when something or someone bumped against the wall. Not in the family room. Laney was almost positive this sound had come from the carport area. That caused the sickening dread to flood through her.

Because it meant there were likely two killers.

Her gun was already raised and ready, but she tried to steady her grip. A shaky hand wasn't going to help them now. Especially since it was possible the two thugs had coordinated an attack. They could come after them at the same time, trapping them in the crossfire.

That put a crushing feeling around her heart to go with the dread that was already there. Owen could be killed. And all because of her. Then these monsters could go upstairs and finish off everyone in the house. That meant she and Owen had to stop them before they got a chance to do that.

Owen's phone dinged, the sound she recognized as a text from Kellan. But Owen didn't take his phone from his pocket. She was thankful for that. Laney didn't want anything to be a distraction right now even though the message could be important.

Laney kept watching. Kept waiting. With her breath so thin, she felt starved for air, and her shoulders so tense, the muscles started to cramp.

She heard another sound. Not footsteps this time but rather a car engine. She didn't risk looking at Owen, but she saw the slash of headlights coming straight for the house.

Kellan.

Maybe.

Eli had told him to stay back to avoid being ambushed. Maybe Kellan had decided against that, which would explain the text to Owen's phone that he hadn't been able to check. If Kellan had indeed decided to come forward, she hoped he wouldn't be shot.

She glanced over her shoulder when the sound and lights got closer. In the distance, Laney could hear the sirens. Too far away to be the vehicle approaching the house.

And it was coming too fast.

There was a loud crash, and it felt as if it shook the entire house. The impact sent the front door flying open, and that was when she realized the car had collided with the front porch.

Maybe this was a third gunman. Or some kind of ruse to distract them from the two who were already in the house. If so, it worked, because the person who staggered through the front door got their attention.

Emerson.

"What the hell is going on?" he grumbled. "The ranch hands wouldn't let me in, and I had to bash through the gate."

The headlights on the car were out now, maybe damaged in the collision, making it was hard to see Emerson in the dark foyer. However, she could tell that he wasn't armed, or rather that he didn't have a gun in his hand, which was probably the only reason Owen hadn't shot him on sight.

Even in the darkness, she noticed that Emerson's eyes widened when he looked at them, and he shook his head as if dazed. Maybe drugged or drunk. Something was definitely wrong.

"What the hell is going on?" Emerson repeated, his words slurred.

"Why are you here?" Owen asked. He had his gun aimed at his brother-in-law while his gaze fired all around the area.

Emerson opened his mouth, closed it and scrubbed his hand over his face. "Something happened to me. I'm not sure what."

Laney had no idea if he was telling the truth, but even if he was, she had no intention of trusting the man. This could all be some trick to make them believe he was innocent when he could be the one pulling the strings on the hired guns. He could have already given them orders to attack.

"Get facedown on the floor," Owen told Emerson. "Put your hands behind your back."

Good. That way, they could maybe restrain him until they could take care of the intruders.

"You're arresting me?" Emerson howled. Now the anger tightened the muscles in his face. "Who the hell do you think you are?"

"I'm the lawman who's going to take you down if you don't get on the floor." There was plenty of anger in Owen's voice, too.

Emerson made a sound of outrage and moved as if he might charge right at them. He didn't get a chance to do that, though, before someone reached out from the side of the stairs and latched onto the man.

Then the person put a gun to Emerson's head.

FROM THE MOMENT Emerson staggered through the door, Owen had figured that things were about to go from bad to worse. He'd thought that maybe Emerson would just start shooting.

Or order his goons to shoot.

And maybe he would still do that, but for now it appeared that one of those hired guns had taken him hostage. *Appeared*, Owen mentally repeated. There was no way he was going to take this at face value.

Owen immediately grasped Laney's arm and pulled her to the side of arched opening that served as an entrance to the family room. As cover went, it wasn't much, so he made sure he was in front of Laney.

"Do anything stupid—*anything*—and the DA dies," the man behind Emerson growled.

Owen didn't recognize the husky voice and, even though it was hard to see the man in the dark shadows, he got a glimpse of part of his face. Owen didn't recognize him, either.

"Let go of me," Emerson yelled and tried to ram his elbow into the gunman's stomach.

The gunman dodged the blow, bashed the butt of his gun against Emerson's head and curved his arm around his neck. Emerson continued to struggle as the man tightened his choke-hold grip.

"What's going on down there?" Eli shouted. "I texted you to tell you that Emerson charged past the hands. Did he make it all the way to the house?"

"Yeah. I'm handling it," Owen answered. "Stay put," he added to his brother when he heard a sound he didn't want to hear.

Addie crying.

"She's okay," Eli quickly said. "The noise just woke her, that's all."

Owen released the breath that had caused the vise-like pressure in his chest. His baby was safe. For now. He needed to make sure she stayed that way.

"Are you working for Emerson?" Owen asked the gunman.

The guy snorted out a laugh. "Does it look like he's my boss?"

A desperate person out to kill them could make this look like anything he wanted. That included setting up a fake hostage situation. But it didn't look fake. Didn't *feel* that way, either. Emerson's head was bleeding, and he was gasping for air. Plus, there was that panicked look in his brother-in-law's eyes, which looked like the real deal.

"Things obviously didn't go as planned," the man said. "My partner's missing. Maybe your sheriff brother took him out, but he's not answering."

That was possibly Kellan's doing or one of the

hands'. Either way, Owen was thankful there was only one of them. But that did make him wonder.

When had it happened?

He'd heard two sets of footsteps—Owen was certain of that—so did that mean Kellan was in the house?

"Because things got screwed up, I need to get out of here, and I'm going to use the DA here to do that," the gunman insisted. "Since it appears he's messed up his car by running it into your porch, I'll be taking that truck parked out front. If you don't have the keys, I'll start shooting, and that woman you're trying to protect just might be the one who takes the bullet."

That sent a shot of anger spearing through Owen. Laney had already been through too much to have this piece of slime threaten her.

"It's okay," Laney whispered to Owen. "Better me than Addie."

He hated that she would even have to consider that. But he was also thankful for it. She was putting his daughter first.

"Give him the keys," Emerson insisted when the man eased up on the choke hold. He sputtered out a cough. "If not, he'll just kill us and take the keys."

Owen stared at him. "You seem pretty cooperative for someone who's being used as a human shield."

Emerson looked Owen straight in the eyes. "I don't want to die. I don't know who's doing this, but we need to get this would-be killer out of the house. My niece is upstairs."

It twisted at Owen to hear Emerson say that. He didn't know if Emerson had genuine concern for Addie the way Laney did or if this was part of the act. Either way, if Emerson left, it would get the gunman away from Addie.

"The truck keys are on the foyer table," Owen told the gunman.

Owen saw the man's gaze immediately go in that direction. The keys were indeed there, and Owen was going to let him take them. Let him go outside, too. And then he would do what he could to stop him so that ambulance could get onto the grounds for Jeremy.

The thug got Emerson moving and he was careful to keep Emerson in front of him. "Take the keys," he growled at Emerson when they reached the foyer table.

Emerson did. His hand closed around the keys just as a shot rang out. For one heart-stopping moment, Owen thought the thug had shot Emerson, but the gunfire had come from the back of the house.

Hell.

The other gunman.

Maybe Kellan hadn't disabled him, after all.

The gunman jerked back, snapping Emerson even closer to him as he put the gun to Emerson's head.

Obviously he didn't think the shot had come from his partner.

"I said I'll kill him, and I sure as hell mean it," the gunman yelled, but he wasn't speaking to Owen. "Stay back or the DA dies."

There was another blast of gunfire.

Then another.

Owen cursed and glanced around, trying to figure out who was doing this. Not Kellan. No. His brother would have called out to them to stop from being shot by friendly fire.

"I think the shooter's near the back stairs," Laney whispered.

That was Owen's guess, too, and it sent his heart to his knees. Because the gunman could be heading up to get to Addie.

"Eli, watch the back stairs," Owen called out to his brother. He knew Eli was already doing that, but he wanted him to have a heads-up.

"Eli won't let a gunman get into the bathroom," Laney reminded him.

Owen believed that. Eli would do whatever it took to protect the little girl, but that didn't mean a gunman couldn't get off a lucky shot.

"I swear I'll kill him," the gunman repeated. With his choke hold still in place, he maneuvered Emerson into the doorway.

Just as there was another shot. This one hadn't come from the back stairs, though. From the sound of it, the gunman had fired from the living room. That meant he was coming closer.

But something wasn't right.

If this was the second gunman, why did the one holding Emerson suddenly look so concerned? Maybe because he thought it was Kellan.

No. It was something else.

"Move," the gunman ordered Emerson. The thug got him onto the porch as another shot came their way. This one slammed into the door frame right next to the gunman's head.

"Stop or I'll kill you," someone said, the voice coming from the living room.

Owen immediately saw the gun the person was holding. Aimed not at Laney and him but rather at the gunman who had Emerson.

And that someone was Nettie.

LANEY INSTANTLY RECOGNIZED Nettie's voice. At first, she thought the woman was there only because she'd followed Emerson. But then she saw Nettie lean out from the arched entry of the living room. One look at her from over Owen's shoulder and Laney knew that Nettie was responsible for the attacks.

Nettie was the person who'd been trying to kill them.

And had maybe murdered Hadley, too.

Emerson shook his head, his expression registering a mix of shock and relief. Then fear. "Nettie, you need to run. This man will kill you."

Nettie definitely didn't run, but she did stay partly behind the cover of the wall. A wall she'd easily be able to duck behind if anyone started shooting.

"Boss," the gunman said, confirming what everyone had already figured out. Everyone but Emerson, that was.

"Boss?" Emerson snapped. "You idiot. That's my wife, and she didn't hire you." He fired some wild-eyed glances at Laney and Owen before his attention settled on Nettie.

Laney saw the realization register on Emerson's face. He groaned. "No. Nettie, not you."

Nettie didn't deny it. "Let go of him, Stan," she ordered the gunman.

Stan was making some wild-eyed glances of his own, and there was fear all over his face. "I don't think that's a good idea. It wasn't my fault he came running in here. He crashed his car into to the porch and just bolted in."

"You should have taken care of the situation before that." Nettie's words were arctic cold and so was the look in her eyes. "Let him go."

So, Nettie was going to save her husband. Maybe. But certainly she didn't think that Emerson and she could just walk out and resume their lives.

"Nettie," Emerson said, his voice cracking. "What have you done? What are you doing?"

"I'm cleaning up your mess. You weren't sup-posed to be here. I told the housekeeper to sneak you a sedative, that you were going off half-cocked and would do something stupid to ruin your career. Your life."

So that was why Emerson had looked drugged. Because he had been.

"I'm trying to fix things," Emerson pled. The gun-man tightened his choke hold when Emerson tried to go to Nettie.

"No, I'm fixing things," Nettie argued. "*Again.* First, with that bimbo you were seeing and now with the mess from those pictures."

"Hadley?" Emerson said. "You knew about Had-ley?"

"Of course I did," Nettie snapped. "She called me crying, and said you'd broken off things with her, but she wanted me to know all about your relation-ship. That's what she called it. A *relationship.* Well, I showed her the price she had to pay for sleeping with my husband. I ended her miserable life."

Oh, mercy. Laney felt as if she'd just been punched in the stomach. Nettie had been the one to murder Hadley. It didn't make it easier, but at least now she knew.

"Damn it, I'm your wife," Nettie snapped, aim-ing a glare at Emerson, "and you cheated on me."

"I'm so sorry." Emerson's eyes shimmered with tears. "God, I'm so sorry."

Nettie dragged in a breath. "I know, and that's the

reason you'll live through this." She looked at Owen now. "But not you. Not Laney. You were smart to tell Eli to stay put, because that means he'll live, too. Or rather, he will, if you cooperate."

"Cooperate how?" Owen's voice was just as cold as hers, and while Laney couldn't see his face, she suspected he matched Nettie glare for glare. "You came here, firing shots, ordering your hired goon to fire shots, and each one of those bullets put my daughter in danger. And why? Because you got your feelings hurt when your husband slept with another woman?"

No more coolness for Nettie. The rage tightened her face and, for the first time, Laney saw the hot emotion that had spurred Nettie to not only kill but to plot to kill again.

"Hadley didn't just sleep with my husband," Nettie growled. She didn't shout, but there was a low, dangerous edge to her voice now. "She tried to blackmail me. Blackmail! I wasn't going to let her get away with that."

"So, you murdered her," Owen said. "And then you killed Joe and Nancy."

Nettie didn't deny that, either. "Cleaning up messes—again." Her mouth went into a flat line. "I didn't know that Nancy had put the pictures on a server."

"How'd Nancy even get the key for the box?" Laney asked.

"From me. I took it that night from Hadley, but I didn't know which bank. It took me a while to find that. But none of this matters. People will forgive Emerson when they learn of the affair."

Laney nearly laughed, and it wasn't from humor. "Do you honestly think that Emerson and you are just going to walk away from this?"

"Yes, because Terrance will get the blame. I've set all of that up." Nettie shifted her attention to Stan, her hired gun. "Let go of my husband."

Stan shook his head. "If I do that, what's to stop you from killing me? You might think of me as part of this mess you want to clean up."

Smart man, because that was no doubt exactly what Nettie was thinking. She could kill Stan, Owen and Laney, and walk out. In Nettie's delusional mind, she might actually believe that everything would be fine.

"Let go of my husband," Nettie repeated and took aim at Stan.

"Nettie," Emerson said, the plea in his voice. "Just please put down your gun. Everyone, put down your guns."

Laney knew that wasn't going to happen. Judging from their expression, so did Stan and Nettie.

"Owen?" Eli called out. "Everything okay down there?"

"Tell him yes," Nettie insisted, her eyes narrowing again. "If you want to save your daughter and him, tell him yes."

Laney could practically feel the debate going on inside Owen. No way did he want to do anything that would risk more gunfire, but even if he did as the woman asked, there were no guarantees that Nettie wouldn't just kill Owen, Stan and her and then go upstairs to do the same.

"Tell Eli yes," Nettie repeated, "or the next shot I fire will go into the ceiling. Maybe into the very room where you're hiding Addie."

Emerson frantically shook his head. "No. You can't do that. Nettie, you can't."

Her expression said otherwise, that she would indeed do the unthinkable.

There were at least fifteen feet of distance between Nettie, Owen and Laney with the foyer and the base of the stairs between them. Emerson and Stan were half that distance. Emerson must have realized he was the one who could get to her first because he rammed his elbow into Stan's stomach. This time, it connected, and the gunman staggered onto the porch before he took off running.

Emerson didn't run.

He launched himself at Nettie.

And the shot blasted through the foyer.

Chapter Sixteen

Owen cursed when he saw what Emerson was about to do, but there had been no time to stop the man. No time, either, to stop the shot that Nettie fired when Emerson lunged toward her.

His brother-in-law made a sharp groan of pain and dropped down right in front of Nettie.

Owen immediately saw the blood spreading across Emerson's chest, and the heard the feral scream that Nettie made. A scream that would almost certainly send Eli running down the stairs if Owen didn't do something about that fast. No way did he want his brother rushing to help. Nettie was still armed and might shoot him.

"Stay put," Owen yelled up to Eli.

Nettie was still screaming, but the sound of Owen's voice must have snagged her attention. She looked at him, her eyes dazed. Maybe in shock. But it didn't last. She took aim at Owen and fired.

Owen shoved Laney back behind the arched

opening. It wasn't good cover since the bullet went straight through a chunk of the drywall, but it was better than nothing.

"This wasn't supposed to happen," Nettie said, her voice a sob now. She was obviously crying. "Oh, God. Emerson wasn't supposed to get shot."

"He needs an ambulance," Owen insisted. "There's one waiting outside. All you have to do is put down your gun and I'll have Kellan send in the EMTs."

"Please," Emerson begged, "do as he says, Nettie. I need help. I'm bleeding out."

Owen glanced over and saw that Nettie, too, was still behind cover, volleying glances between Emerson and him. Emerson was clutching his stomach, moaning in pain, and yes, he was bleeding out.

Nettie shook her head, obviously trying to decide what to do. If she saved her husband, the man she supposedly loved enough to kill for, then she would be arrested for multiple murders and the attacks.

"I love you, Nettie," Emerson added. Maybe he did. Or maybe Emerson was just trying to do the right thing and calm Nettie enough to get her to put down that gun.

"I can't go to jail," Nettie said. Owen could hear the panic in her voice. "I can't live without you."

Emerson tried to speak but his eyelids fluttered down.

"No!" Nettie yelled and fired a shot at Owen. "He's dead. He can't be dead."

"He's not," Owen assured her while he glanced out from behind cover. He kept his attention nailed to Nettie. "Look at his chest. You can see he's still breathing."

Owen had no idea if that was true. Emerson could indeed be dead, but if so, there was nothing Owen could do about it. However, he could do something about Nettie. He got that chance when the woman hurried to her husband. That was all Owen needed.

"Put down your gun, Nettie," Owen warned a split second before he stepped out and took aim at her.

Nettie shrieked, bringing up her own gun, and he saw the madness and rage in her eyes. She was going to kill him. Or rather, she would try. And that was why Owen made sure he pulled the trigger first.

He sent two shots slamming into Nettie's chest.

Laney stepped out to Owen's side and pointed her gun at Nettie. But the woman wasn't down. Despite the bullets Owen had put in her, Nettie might have gotten off another shot—at Owen—but Emerson caught Nettie's leg and dragged her down to the floor with him.

Owen rushed toward them, ripping Nettie's gun from her hand and passing it back to Laney. He didn't want to give Nettie another chance to kill them. But the woman had maybe given up on that. Sobbing, bleeding, she pulled Emerson into her arms.

Despite his heartbeat pounding in his ears, Owen still heard the footsteps and automatically pivoted in their direction at the top of the stairs. It was Eli, who cursed when he looked at the bloodbath in the foyer.

"The gunman ran," Owen relayed to his brother. "He could still be somewhere on the grounds."

"I'll go up and stand guard outside Addie's door," Laney offered.

Owen hated to put her in the position where she might have to defend herself, and his child, but he preferred that to sending her out to look for a hired gun. He nodded, wishing he could say more to her, but he would save that for later. Later, when he was certain there was no chance of another attack.

Eli and Laney passed each other on the stairs as his brother came down. Eli took out his phone. To call Kellan, Owen quickly realized.

"I'll look for the gunman and check on Jeremy," Eli offered. "But I won't go far," his brother added as he hurried out the front door.

Owen didn't put his gun away in case Stan returned, but he went closer to Emerson and Nettie and tried to figure out what to do to save them. Not that he especially wanted to save Nettie, but he would try. There was no way, though, that he could tamp down the hatred he felt for her. She'd not only tried to kill him, Nettie had endangered plenty of people who he loved.

Including Laney.

That realization came out of the blue and hit him damn hard. But he shoved it away and used his left hand to apply some pressure to the wound on Emerson's chest. There wasn't much he could do for Nettie. The gravelly rale coming from her throat let him know that she was on her last breath.

"I'm sorry," Emerson said. "I swear I didn't know she was behind this. I didn't know she had planned all of this or I would have stopped her." He grimaced, groaning in pain. "I thought it was Terrance."

So had Owen. Or at least, Terrance had been one of their suspects but so had Emerson and Nettie. And Nettie had planned to use Terrance's suspect status to frame him for the murders and attacks.

Owen whirled around at the sound of yet more approaching footsteps—these coming from the front yard.

"It's me," Kellan called out to him.

Owen didn't allow himself to relax because there were still too many things that could go wrong. But he was glad when his brother came rushing in.

Kellan glanced around, as Eli had done, clearly assessing the situation before his attention settled on Emerson and Nettie.

"Nettie did this," Emerson said and started crying when he looked at Nettie, realizing that she was gone.

"Nettie did all of this," Owen added. "She confessed to killing Hadley, Joe and Nancy. She hired the gunmen. And she was going to set up Terrance."

Kellan nodded. "Eli just cuffed one of her guys.

Said his name was Stan Martin. He's talking in case we need any more info."

Good. But Owen figured they wouldn't need more. Not with Nettie dead.

"How's Jeremy?" Owen asked.

"He's not hurt too bad. He'll need to go to the hospital, but it can wait for a little while."

Kellan motioned to someone outside and several moments later two EMTs came rushing in. Owen stepped back so they could start to work on Emerson. He was still bleeding, but he was very much alive, and that was more than Owen could say for Nettie.

"If you've got this, I need to check on Addie and the others. Laney," Owen said under his breath. "I need to check on her."

Kellan gave him the go-ahead while he stooped down to talk to Emerson. Owen heard Kellan read him his rights. A necessity because even though it didn't appear Emerson had anything to do with the murders, he'd still obstructed justice and lied during an interview. It might not land him in jail, but it was almost certainly going to cost him his legal license and his job.

It seemed to take forever for Owen to make his way up the stairs. His legs, and heart, felt heavy, and there was still way too much adrenaline pumping through him. That lightened a little when he spotted Laney. She was exactly where he'd expected to find her, standing guard outside the bedroom door.

She looked at him, their gazes immediately connecting, and he saw the relief in her eyes when she ran to him. "Addie's okay," she said. "They're all okay. I just checked on them, and Addie's fallen back asleep."

Owen pulled her into his arms and another layer of that heaviness vanished. With all the shots that had been fired, it was somewhat of a miracle they hadn't been killed.

"Nettie?" she asked, easing back.

"Dead."

He paused to let her absorb that and everything else that went along with it. The woman who'd made their lives a living hell was gone. Now they had to deal with the aftermath and the nightmares.

Laney shook her head. "I'm sorry I didn't see sooner that Nettie was the one. I was looking too hard at Emerson to realize the truth."

Owen sighed. Leave it to Laney to apologize for not recognizing a jealous woman hell-bent on covering up her husband's affair. Because he didn't want her apology, or for Laney to feel regretful in any way for this, he brushed a kiss on her mouth.

She definitely didn't melt against him, didn't give him one of those smoldering looks. Her reaction was that tears sprang to her eyes. So Owen kissed her again. This time he heard that slight hitch in her throat and thought maybe there was a little melting going on. This time when she pulled back, he definitely saw some.

Felt some, too.

Laney gave him a small smile, one he figured took a lot of effort on her part. "I'll be okay. I'll just wait out here while you see Addie."

A few days ago, he would have taken her up on that offer. But since this was now, tonight, he slipped his arm around her and opened the bedroom door.

"It's me," Owen called out. "You can unlock the bathroom door."

Seconds later, he heard someone do just that. He also heard mutterings of relief. Saw relief, too, on Gemma's and Francine's faces when Gemma opened the door. The face that he didn't see was Addie's. But he soon spotted his little girl asleep on a quilt inside the tub.

"Don't go downstairs. Not yet," Owen instructed the women. "Kellan's down there, and he's fine," he added to Gemma.

Clearly relieved, Gemma gave him a hard hug and went into the bedroom to look out the door and into the hall. He was betting she would wait right there until Kellan came up for her.

"The gunman is dead?" Francine whispered and then checked over her shoulder to make sure Addie hadn't heard. She hadn't.

"Arrested." Owen had to pause again. "Nettie's dead, though. She's the one who did this."

Owen figured in the next few hours, Francine would learn a lot more about what had gone on. Everyone in Longview Ridge would. But, for now, that was enough information.

Francine went to the bed and sank onto the foot of it. She didn't come out and say it, but Owen figured she'd done that to give him some alone time with Addie. He wanted that, but he took Laney's hand to make sure that "alone time" included her, too.

Owen sat on the floor next to the tub, easing Laney down with him. He didn't want to wake Addie, but he had to brush his fingers over her cheek and hair. She stirred a little but settled right back down.

"I hope she won't remember any of this," Laney whispered.

That was his hope, too, but he would certainly remember it in crystal clear detail. Both the bad and the good. Because plenty of good had come out of this, too—including what had happened between him and Laney just a couple of hours earlier in the room across the hall.

Owen wanted to hang on to that, but when he looked at Laney, he saw yet another apology in her eyes. Tears, too. This time he didn't sigh. He huffed and hauled Laney onto his lap.

"This wasn't your fault. There's no reason for you to be sorry." With that, he kissed her again. This time it wasn't just to hush her but because he needed to feel her in his arms. Needed his mouth on hers.

And that was what he got.

He felt it. Not just the heat, though, but also the feelings that went deeper than just the lust. He felt everything for her that he hadn't been sure he could ever feel again. Yet, here it was. Here she was, right on his lap and kissing him back.

This time when he pulled back, he didn't see a trace of an apology. Thankfully, didn't see any tears, either, so that meant the kiss had done its job. Now he wanted to carry it one step further.

"I love you," Laney blurted before he could say anything. "I know, you'll probably think it's too soon, that you're not ready for it, but I can't change what I feel for you. For Addie," she added, glancing at the baby. "I love you both, and even if that sends you running, I wanted you to know."

Owen opened his mouth but still didn't get a chance to say anything.

"Please don't run," she whispered, pressing her forehead to his. "Just give it a chance and see where it goes."

"No," he said. This time he saw the flash of surprise and hurt in her eyes, and that was why he continued—quickly, "I don't need to give it a chance. Don't need to see where it's going, because it's going exactly where I want."

Laney blinked, shifted back enough so she could study his face. She smiled a little. "To bed?"

"Absolutely. The bed…and other places."

Her smile widened and she kissed him. It went on

a lot longer and became a lot deeper than Owen had planned because he hadn't finished what he'd wanted to say. That was why he broke away.

"Other places like my house," he said. "That I hope you can think of as your house, too."

Laney's smile faded. "You're asking me to move in with you?"

"I'm asking for a whole lot more than that. I'm in love with you, Laney."

She froze, her eyes widening, and for one heart-stopping moment, he thought she was going to say that she didn't believe him. But then she threw herself back into his arms and gave him an amazing kiss. One that told him that this was exactly what she wanted, too.

Now it was Owen who smiled. For a few seconds anyway, but the movement in the tub had both of them looking at Addie. She was no longer asleep. She sat up, looked at them. And grinned.

"Da-da," she said, reaching for him.

Laney and he reached over and pulled her from the tub. Holding both Laney and his daughter, Owen knew that he had exactly what he wanted in his arms.

* * * * *

Look for more books in USA TODAY
*bestselling author Delores Fossen's
Longview Ridge Ranch miniseries
later this year.*

*And don't miss the previous title in the
Longview Ridge Ranch series,* Safety Breach,
available now from Harlequin Intrigue!

YOU HAVE
JUST READ A
HARLEQUIN®
INTRIGUE®
BOOK

If you were **captivated** by the **gripping, page-turning romantic suspense,** be sure to look for all six Harlequin® Intrigue® books every month.

HARLEQUIN®
INTRIGUE

COMING NEXT MONTH FROM

H HARLEQUIN

INTRIGUE

Available January 21, 2020

#1905 WITNESS PROTECTION WIDOW
A Winchester, Tennessee Thriller • by Debra Webb
In witness protection under a new name, Allison James, aka the Widow, must work together with her ex-boyfriend, US Marshal Jaxson Stevens, to outsmart her deceased husband's powerful crime family and bring justice to the group.

#1906 DISRUPTIVE FORCE
A Declan's Defenders Novel • by Elle James
Assassin CJ Grainger has insider knowledge about the terrorist organization Trinity after escaping the group. With help from Cole McCastlain, a member of Declan's Defenders, can she stop Trinity before its plan to murder government officials is executed?

#1907 CONFLICTING EVIDENCE
The Mighty McKenzies Series • by Lena Diaz
Peyton Sterling knows she can only prove her brother's innocence by working with US Marshal Colin McKenzie, even though he helped put her brother in jail. Yet in their search for the truth, they'll unearth secrets that are more dangerous than they could have imagined...

#1908 MISSING IN THE MOUNTAINS
A Fortress Defense Case • by Julie Anne Lindsey
Emma Hart knows her ex-boyfriend's security firm is the only group she can trust to help her find her abducted sister. But she's shocked when her ex, Sawyer Lance, is the one who comes to her aid.

#1909 HER ASSASSIN FOR HIRE
A Stealth Novel • by Danica Winters
When Zoey Martin's brother goes missing, she asks her ex, black ops assassin Eli Wayne, for help. With a multimillion-dollar bounty on Zoey's brother's head, they won't be the only ones looking for him, and some people would kill for that much money...

#1910 THE FINAL SECRET
by Cassie Miles
On her first assignment as a bodyguard for ARC Security, former army corps member Genevieve "Gennie" Fox and her boss, former SEAL Noah Sheridan, must solve the murder he has been framed for.

HICNM0120

Get 4 FREE REWARDS!

We'll send you 2 FREE Books plus 2 FREE Mystery Gifts.

Harlequin Intrigue® books feature heroes and heroines that confront and survive danger while finding themselves irresistibly drawn to one another.

FREE
Value Over
$20

Love Harlequin romance?

DISCOVER.

Be the first to find out about promotions, news and exclusive content!

Facebook.com/HarlequinBooks

Twitter.com/HarlequinBooks

Instagram.com/HarlequinBooks

Pinterest.com/HarlequinBooks

ReaderService.com

EXPLORE.

Sign up for the Harlequin e-newsletter and download a free book from any series at **TryHarlequin.com.**

CONNECT.

Join our Harlequin community to share your thoughts and connect with other romance readers!
Facebook.com/groups/HarlequinConnection

HARLEQUIN®

**ROMANCE WHEN
YOU NEED IT**

HSOCIAL2018